Kathy

Enjoy

FAMILY LOVE AND BETRAYAL

E.A. Gordanier

E.A. GORDANIER

Book Trailer
https://www.facebook.com/onthe
waypublishing/videos/727698538/
60578/?extid=CL-UNK-UNK-UNK-AN_
GKOT-GK1C

ON THE WAY
EDITING & PUBLISHING

COPYRIGHT

© 2020 On The Way Publishing

All rights reserved. No part of this publication may be reproduced, distributed, or transmitted in any form or by any means, including photocopying, recording, or other electronic or mechanical methods, without the prior written permission of the publisher, except in the case of brief quotations embodied in critical reviews and certain other non-commercial uses permitted by copyright law. For permission requests, write to the publisher, addressed "Attention: Permissions Coordinator," at the address below.

ISBN e-book: 978-1-990080-09-8

ISBN paperback: 978-1-990080-10-4

ISBN hardback: 978-1-990080-11-1

Editors: **Rhonda Chieduch, Debbie Kensington**

Cover Artist: Randy Smith

Publisher: On the Way Editing & Publishing

4755 47 Street, Onoway, AB TOE 1VO Canada

otwep20@gmail.com

1

HELGA

This morning begins like every other morning. I am awakened by the peaceful sounds of starlings perched on my windowsill. These birds are incredibly pretty with their iridescent plumage shimmering in shades of dark green and brown. I love being serenaded by my feathery friends.

"Good morning to you my beautiful, feathered friends. How are you all doing today?"

I always leave my window open a crack. The fresh air is soothing and mimics a gentle massage on my skin. The outside of my windows is streaked by my pathetic attempt to clean them. The sun casts a kaleidoscope of colors on my walls and any object fortunate to be in the beams' way. I hold out my arm and it becomes a rainbow of colors as the beams radiate and bounce off my arm. I am mesmerized at the beauty of these colors. What a beautiful magical way to begin the morning. I lie back on my bed and place my hands behind my head. I close my eyes and drift into solitude listening to the symphony of my birds and feeling the sun soothing my skin.

Suddenly, I hear the roar of engines piercing the calmness and serenity of the sky. This loud noise startles my sacred symphony which is replaced by the flutter of their wings. I look out my window and see a plane flying low over my neighborhood. Is it the Dutch air force working on a solo drill?

After a few seconds, I hear a loud deafening explosion quickly followed by three others. The blasts rattle our house and windows and I hear the sound of breaking glass on the main floor. My heart is racing, and my breathing is labored as my body goes into flight or fight mode. My ears are deafened by the explosions. I drop to the bedroom floor and cover my head with my hands to protect myself against any broken glass or debris. I am frozen in time, afraid to move! As I listen to my racing heart beating to escape the terror, I realize that several minutes have passed.

My mother's screams echo throughout the house.

"Helga, are you safe?"

"Yes Mother, I am safe."

I take a chance, not knowing if another series of explosions will occur, and crawl over to my window and peer out of it. The sky is filled with thick choking smoke and there is an infernal of angry blood red flames shooting into the sky. I close my window to keep the toxic smoke out of my lungs. I look out the window and I see that the lone Dutch elm tree in our yard has lost all of its beautiful young leaves in the explosion. Its leaves have defensively fallen to the ground from the tree shaking to the vibration of the bombs.

As I quickly throw on my knee length navy blue dress I wonder if the gates of Hell have opened. I race down the stairs, taking two steps at a time. I run into the parlor and am greeted by my hysterical mother. I look out the parlor window and can still see the angry blood red flames and the suffocating thick black smoke aggressively inching its way across the sky toward us. The shocks from the bombs have jarred my mother's china cabinet door open and several of her mother's prized pieces of crystal have shattered on the floor.

Lukasz, our gardener, and Olga, our housekeeper, are standing by mother. Everyone, including myself, look frantic and frightened. I give them both a hug and say a prayer to God underneath my breath. Although Lukasz and Olga both work for us, they are treated as members of our family.

I sit on the small cream-colored French boudoir sofa. I look at mother who is shaking like the Dutch elm tree in our front yard while trying to sweep up her once prized crystal pieces. I realize that I have to be the rational one during this crisis. Mother, God bless her, is the emotional one in the family who will burst into tears at the slightest deviation from the norm.

Speaking in a concerned voice I say to mother, "Mother, please sit down, you are making me nervous."

The lights flicker in the darkened sky. Mother reaches for the telephone and is surprised that it is working. Within seconds after her hanging it up it rings, making us all jump. Mother answers the telephone, and it is father, Dr. Lars Vand Der Beak.

"Lars, what is happening?" Mother asks nervously.

"Darling, the Nazis have dropped 4 bombs in Amsterdam. These bombs fell on the Herengracht area, 1.5 km from our home. The ambulances and citizens are bringing in injured individuals. Is everyone safe there?"

"Yes Lars, Olga and Lukasz both came inside when the bombing started. They were in the garden picking vegetables for dinner. They are safe but very shaken."

My mom holds the phone out and my father speaks up so that we can all hear. "Great. Ok darling, I want you, Olga, and Lukasz to move food supplies, containers of water, medical supplies, and bedding down into the cellar. We must be prepared, just in case there is another bombing. I want Helga to have the radio on and listen for any updates. Darling, I must get back to work. I will be home as soon as I can, I love you."

"We love you too," mother screeches in a hysterical voice.

After mother finishes speaking with father, she collapses onto her lavender French boudoir sofa. She reaffirms what father has told her about the Nazis in case we didn't hear him. I turn the radio on loud and help carry supplies into our cellar. Our cellar is big, roomy enough for all five of us. Father and I both know that if our house experiences a direct hit, we will all be dead. Our house is old and the cellar ceiling is not reinforced with extra bracing. The wooden structure will not withstand a direct hit. The temperature in the cellar is cooler than the rest of the house. The cellar is already being used to house our canned goods and father's exquisite wine collection, complete with corkscrews. Great, if we are prisoners in our cellar, we can at least get drunk on expensive wine!

We three ladies begin to descend the stairs to the cellar with our arms full of food, medicine, bedding and other supplies that will make our lives semi comfortable if we need to escape to the cellar. Our auditory senses are on high alert as we try to discern any sounds both inside and outside the house. The cellar is not sound-proof and it seems as if we hear every creak the house expresses. I didn't realize that our house was so noisy. Lukasz, who lives in the small house in the rear of the garden, is out collecting his meager possessions. He brings in one armful of his supplies that he thinks will be vital to our survival. Olga brings down pictures of her childhood in St. Petersburg, Russia. Everyone has their own secret reason for what treasures and survival items they bring into the cellar.

As we make numerous trips to the cellar, Olga offers to make us tea and cuts us each of us a slice of her freshly made appeltaart served with a dollop of met slagroom.

"Thank you, Olga, your appeltaart and met slagroom are amazing." I smile as I compliment her baking. For a Russian lady, she makes the best Dutch food.

I go back down to the cellar to help organize our treasures and survival items. I begin to hyperventilate and feel the walls closing in on me. I need to escape from the cellar. It is going to collapse! I quickly ascend the stairs and try to relax. I need to keep busy above the cellar. It is amazing how quickly and seductively your mind likes to play tricks on you. I guess it is the fear of the unknown that terrorizes my mind. Mother gives me a big hug and tells me to help Olga in the kitchen.

I jump as I hear a key turning in our front door. Mother quickly ascends from the cellar as she is aware that father is the only other person who has a key to our house. Mother collapses in his arms and I can hear her whisper in his ear, "Lars I need you. Why is this happening?"

Father, with his arms around Mother, escorts her to the sofa.

"Mr. Lars I am glad you are safe." Olga and Lukasz say simultaneously.

"Thank you. Please, let me join you for tea and I will update you on the situation."

Father is wearing a clean hospital jacket and has a look of terror in his eyes.

Before he can say anything, mother blurts out, "Has the bombing stopped?"

"Berta, please relax. We are ok. We are alive. Others are not as fortunate. We must be thankful. The bombing has stopped. Please do not go outside for any reason. I will bring home any extra medicine I can get from the hospital. I love you all and will return back home as soon as I can. We are very busy at the hospital due to all the bomb related injuries."

Father eats and drinks quickly and leaves for the hospital for God knows how long. After he leaves we sit around the radio in the parlor, listening for news. We all lean forward as we hear Queen Wilhelmina's voice come on the radio.

"The Herengracht area of Amsterdam has been bombed by a German Junkers Ju 88 bomber. There are 44 confirmed dead and 79 injured. I have consulted with the military and they are on alert both defensively and offensively for German aggressiveness. Please stay calm and we will update you when necessary. May God bless our people, our country, and our flag."

CHAPTER TWO

T oday is May 12, 1940, one day after the Nazis dropped four bombs on Amsterdam; four bombs that were close to our house. I feel as though my once peaceful life has been shattered by the aggressive evil Nazis. Although father instructed mother and I to stay indoors, I know that he would approve of me checking on our neighbors Mr. and Mrs. Katz. I tell mother that I want to check on the Katzes and she nods in approval. Mr. and Mrs. Katz are our Jewish neighbors. They live in their grandparents' house with three generations residing in their beautiful home. Grandmother Katz, who has a weak heart lives on the main floor in their home. Elishva, their 12-year-old daughter has a beautiful bedroom on the second floor with windows overlooking the canal. Mr. Katz owns a lucrative trade business which he inherited from his father, who inherited it from his.

We have celebrated many Jewish festivals with them. They obey the Sabbath which begins just before sundown on Friday. I have been at their home when the Sabbath is marked by the lighting of the shabbat candles and the recitation of Kiddush over a cup of wine. Mrs. Katz informed me that the Sabbath concludes Saturday night with a prayer known as Havdalah. My family is not Jewish, but we respect their culture and Mrs. Katz has taught me Yiddish. We, in turn, have invited the Katz family to our house for Christmas dinner and to celebrate the birth of Jesus Christ.

It is interesting how we both respect each other's faith and embrace our friendship.

I run across our yards and pound on their front door. Sarah, their housekeeper, answers the door and I ask if everyone is safe.

"Yes, everyone is safe Ms. Helga. Please come in."

Mrs. Katz greets me and embraces me in a big hug before saying, "Thank you for checking on us Ms. Helga. Mr. Katz is safe at work and Elishva is completing her school assignments".

I look down at Mrs. Katz's belly and notice it is getting bigger. Her baby is due in September and they hope for a healthy baby boy, or a girl, for Elishva. We chat for a few minutes and I try to reassure her, and myself, that we are safe.

I return home and find mother assisting Olga with dinner preparation. There are four place settings on the table. It will not be the first time that father is absent for dinner, but it is the first time he will be absent during a dangerous situation.

In the morning, we try to get the normalcy back into our lives. I defy father and mother and slip outside. I follow the road beside the Herengracht canal to the bombed area and am mortified at the destruction in front of me. Many houses are reduced to smoldering ash and several have partial walls standing in isolation. Us Dutch people are very resilient and will help fellow Dutchmen or Dutchwomen who are in distress. I speak to a Dutch policeman and ask him if any of the families need assistance.

"I am not sure. Everyone has been assigned a temporary residence and once the debris has been cleared, the rebuilding with begin. From what I understand, many of the families have been assisted by family members. If you want, I will take your name and telephone number to give to the committee members helping the families."

It is May 13, 1940, we are sitting in the living room listening to the radio. It is announced on the radio that the Royal Family and senior government officials have fled the Netherlands and will be living in exile in London. In the Queen's absence, General Westenberg is the acting most senior authority in the country on both military and civilian matters.

Angerly I blurt out, "How can she abandon us at a time like this?"

"Helga, bite your tongue. I thought I have taught you better, our

Dutch Queen has not abandoned us. Can you imagine what would happen to them if the Nazis got their hands on them? I know, deep down that she will lead us and advise us from afar. She is an honorable woman."

"I am sorry mother, but I am frightened."

"I know Helga, but us Dutch are strong people, so are Olga and Lukasz. We will get through this. We just need to be smart."

Underneath my breath, I pray to God to protect us.

CHAPTER THREE

Today, May 14, 1940, mother and I are busy in our house. Mother has a professional dressmaking room to the right of our foyer. She is an accomplished dressmaker and has designed and made gowns for many of the who's who in Amsterdam. Now that I am a grown woman she frequently requests me to model these gowns while she puts on the finishing touches on her creations. I feel like a princess when I see my reflection in her floor length mahogany mirror. Mother is busy sewing a navy-blue gown for the mayor's wife. I look at mother's creation and I comment to her that if the mayor's wife does not like the gown, I will keep it. Mother gives me a loving smile.

After helping Mother, I go into the parlor. I sit and begin to practice speaking and writing German before focusing on Russian. I attend the University of Amsterdam and am studying foreign languages and culture. I am fluent in Yiddish, German, Dutch, English, French, Polish, and Russian. The last two languages I have known since I was a little girl as our housekeeper is Russian and our gardener is Polish. I must not forget my neighbors, the Katzes, who are Jewish and have taken the time to teach me their language and customs as well. I am honored to have these individuals in my life and privileged that they share their language, customs, and intimate details of their lives with me.

Since the bombing of Amsterdam, Mother has diligently blasted our radio on high. I try to tune the radio out while working on my languages, but I am listening intuitively for updates on the Nazis. I put on a brave face but deep down I know that I am frightened of the unknown. I have an uneasy feeling in my stomach. My stomach feels as it if is twisted into a knot. I feel impending doom and I cannot shake this feeling.

Suddenly the radio crackles and the announcer screams, "The Nazis have bombed Rotterdam and the city center is ablaze. There are reports of fatalities and causalities and further updates will be broadcasted as we get additional information."

Mother and I, along with Olga and Lukasz, are speechless. We pray for the victims, our Queen, and our country. Mother is beside herself.

"Mother, I know this is devastating but we need to remain calm. I will listen to the radio for any updates. I think you should continue working on Ms. Van der Beef's dress. It will keep you busy."

"Yes, Helga, you are correct."

I pour Mother a cup of tea that Olga has prepared for us and hand it to her. She takes it and quickly scurries into her dressmaking room, frightened and confused.

It seems that every five minutes there are updates on the bombing. The radio waves are vibrating with the devastating news. The Dutch military has been decimated. Rotterdam has 1000 dead civilians, 1000's injured, and there are 18,000 civilians that are homeless. The Nazis mercilessly bombed civilian areas: homes, churches, and schools fell like dominos! The St. Lawrence is the only remaining building reminiscent of Rotterdam's medieval architecture.

Father calls around 16:00 and informs us that he will not be coming home for dinner. They will be busy with the casualties coming in from the Rotterdam bombing. He also states that he will get reliable information from the injured soldiers who will be trickling into the hospital. Father speaks to Mother and I and reinforces that we stay calm and diligent as the Nazis are. Father also relays the same message to Olga and Lukasz.

After we have finished speaking to Father, Mother slowly walks back to her dressmaking room and I sit on the sofa with my head in my hands. I am shaking with fear and anger! I remember what Father told us when Amsterdam was first bombed.

"Do not trust the Nazis! They have secretly disobeyed the Vienna Conference and have rebuilt their military. I have read Mein Kompf and it is clear that Hitler is mercilessly seeking world domination. First there was Austria, Poland, and Czechoslovakia. Now we are on his radar. The lessons of World War 1 should be etched in our minds."

"Mother, I want to check on the Katzes again to make sure they are ok."

"OK, Helga, please be careful."

"Mother they live beside us."

"I know Helga, but I am worried about our Jewish neighbors."

I open the front door and search for anyone walking or driving by. I have read Mein Kompf and I am aware that the Jews are not well respected by the Nazis. I put my scarf over my head and walk up the walkway to their house. Their house is similar to ours. I knock on the door and Sarah; the housekeeper slowly opens the door. She recognizes me and pulls me inside while scanning the area for any individuals lurking nearby. Mrs. Katz is in the kitchen but quickly gets up and comes over to give me a hug.

I speak first and tell her that we are worried about her and her family. She motions for me to sit on one of the sofas. Their house is beautifully decorated with magnificent original art, crystal, and gorgeous furniture with intricate Italian lace. My favorite paintings are *The Hague Forest with a View of Huis ten Bosch Palace* by Joris Van der Haagan and *The Concert* by Johannes Vermeer.

"Miss Helga, we are very frightened. We have heard rumors of what has been happening to Jewish people in other occupied areas in Poland. My gosh, our family has been in the Netherlands for hundreds of years. I pray that his hate will not transfer here," Mrs. Katz says in a concerned voice.

After my meeting with Mrs. Katz, I am extremely worried about what is in store for all of us. Olga has set the table for five people and I am happy that Father will be joining us for dinner. I watch in surprise as this 'gentleman' gobbles down his meal as if he has not eaten in weeks. As we retire to the parlor to listen to the radio at a lower decibel, a familiar voice comes over the airwaves; it is General Westenberg and he has a proclamation for the Dutch citizens.

"This afternoon Germany bombarded Rotterdam, while Utrecht has also been threatened with destruction. In order to spare the civil population and to prevent further bloodshed I feel myself justified in ordering all troops concerned to suspend operations. By great superiority of the most modern means the Nazis have succeeded in breaking our resistance. We have nothing wherewith to reproach ourselves in connection with this war. Your bearing, and that of the forces was calm, firm of purpose and worthy of the Netherlands. We have surrendered to the Nazis."

A feeling of hopelessness and doom penetrates the room

CHAPTER FOUR

I t is May 15, 1940 and Mother, Father, and I are sipping tea while our ears focus on any crackle or verbal sound that our radio emits. We anticipate that it is just a matter of time before Hitler dominates our Dutch airwaves and just like that the devil interrupts our afternoon tea. He poisons our Dutch airwaves with an announcement that Ared Schwarz is now the Reich Commissariat for the Occupied Dutch Territories. Shortly after his announcement, Ared Schwarz dominates the Dutch airwaves and promises the shocked Dutch population that things will return to normal. In addition, he stresses that it will be simple; all the Dutch population has to do is obey all the rules that he will be implementing. If any of these rules are disobeyed, there will be severe repercussions. Both of the speeches are short and to the point; we are under Nazi control!

When I hear these vile words, I look at the radio and yell ""Fuck you Nazi bastards! Mother and Father's mouths drop as if they both have consumed a stinging insect. I know that they are in shock from my choice of words. Meanwhile, Olga and Lukasz both smile and wink at me before I storm out of the parlor, stomp up the wooden stairs, and fiercely slam my bedroom door. I am very angry! I attempt to punch the life out of my pillow. How dare that Ared character say things will get back to normal! You Nazis bombed my city and Rotterdam and killed scores of people. You Nazis attacked civilians, heartless cruel bastards! My tears are flowing out of my swollen eyes and flooding the crevasses in my pillow. My anger puts me into fighting mode. My heart is racing and feels like it desperately wants to escape the impending terror that the Nazis will impose on us. I am tense and trembling from fear of the unknown. I gasp for air as I feel my bronchial tree tightening its grip in my chest, trying to suffocate me. I take deep breaths of air, trying to get it into the tightened airways and try to calm down. Easier said than done.

As I try to reduce my anxiety, I hear several gentle knocks on my bedroom door. I recognize the knock; it belongs to a concerned kind-hearted Father. Before I answer the door, I make an honest attempt to compose myself. I know that my eyes are bloodshot, and my hair looks like a rat's nest. I look in the mirror and see from my reflection that I look like I have been through a war zone. Correction, I am living in a war zone!

"Yes Father, please come in."

As he opens the door, he inspects the door hinge and checks for any damage, "Mmm everything is intact, by the way you slammed your bedroom door I thought that Lukasz would have to fix your door." He looks at my mangled pillow and asks if it is still alive?

We both lightly laugh and then Father sits beside me on the bed and puts his arm around me. "Helga, I understand your frustration. I understand where the hate for the Nazis comes from. The Nazis will tighten their grip on us and try to oppress us until we bow to Hitler for mercy. We must be smart and not trust the Nazis. They will try to be kind and respectful, but we both know they have a hidden agenda. It is important to keep our emotions in check and function as best as we can in this situation."

"Father, I worry about Mother."

"Helga, she will be fine. I know that she is easily excitable, but she is at her best when she is focusing on her dressmaking. Plus, I have been giving her half a sedative that calms down her erratic behavior yet still allows her to function halfway normal. What I mean is that she is still able to work on dresses. Helga, one thing to keep in mind is that Mother is making a dress for Mayor Daan's wife. I know that your mother will have several fittings with her. When she is over for her fittings, we can ask her questions about the Nazis. I know that her husband discusses in detail daily events and any future plans in our municipal government over dinner. I believe deep down that Mr. Daan Vossem, our mayor, is not a Nazi supporter, but he has to put on a facade to appease the powers that be."

I look up at Father and he has a grin on his face that goes from ear to ear.

"Helga, we must adapt to this situation. If you recall what Charles Darwin said Survival of the Fittest."

"Yes, Father, we will adapt and survive."

After Father leaves my bedroom, I go into the lavatory to freshen up. I comb and untangle the rat's nest out of my hair. My eyes are still swollen and red. I know that no amount of makeup will soften the puffiness around them. Oh well, I can't be beautiful every day! After I freshen up, I follow Father downstairs and apologize for my unladylike behavior. Mother is taking a nap on our teak sofa that has a wavy back, paw feet, and rattan peach upholstery.

CHAPTER FIVE

L ater on that day, General Westenberg signs the Capitulation of the Netherlands. Immediately the Nazi's Reich Minister of Propaganda's begins to infect the Dutch airwaves. The airwaves are inundated with lies and mores lies to oppress the morale and spirit of Dutch citizens. The Nazi propaganda machine ridicules the Dutch royal family for rejecting Hitler's offer for protection under the Third Reich. The Nazis further capitalize on how The Dutch royal family, Prime Minister Van Oorschot and members of his cabinet abandon the Dutch people and country in their time of need. These lies will not oppress me as I am a strong wise Dutch woman!

In reality, Prime Minister Van Oorschot may be physically absent from the Netherlands; but he is with us over the airwaves. He announces in his speech (commentary op de Aanwijzingen) the guidelines on how public servants are expected to behave. He stresses that public servants are not to co-operate with the occupying forces or assist in any way in the oppression and deportation of Jews and other members of Dutch society that have fallen out of favor with the Nazis.

Father, Mother, Olga, Lukasz and I sit around the radio and listen to his speech which is repeatedly broadcast on the Dutch airwaves. Everyone, except Mother, applauds during Prime Minister's Van Oorschot 's speech. Mother looks as though she is going to burst into tears; her bottom lip is quivering. Mother is the type of woman who prefers life in a structured manner and does not cope well when her life spirals out of control. Father, being a good husband and doctor gives her a sedative when she becomes too dramatic, like right now!

"Lars, how can he help us when he is safe in London?" Mother shrieks at Father.

Oh my, here we go again. I love my mother dearly, but her attitude and outlook on life is starting to deteriorate my soul. Father, the optimist in the family, attempts to reassure her that our family is strong, and we will get through this together. I know that Father is lying through his teeth, but he has to defuse the bomb, which in this case is Mother, before she explodes. Thank God for sedatives.

Father excuses himself and gently nudges me towards the kitchen. As we walk into the kitchen he states, "Although the government is trying to guide us from afar, in reality, we have to deal with the Nazis on a daily basis." Again, he reinforces that the Nazis cannot be trusted. "We must be careful with whom we speak to and what we say. Helga, we have both read and analyzed Mein Kompf together. Hitler is a madman. He is a metastatic cancer that secretly spreads to unexpecting territories and countries."

I nod in agreement.

6

ARED SCHWARTZ

After the official Copulation of the Netherlands, I quickly hand pick my puppet regime.

I think I will keep several Dutch officials in their offices, for now. My first meeting will be with the Mayor of Amsterdam, Daan Vossem. Prior to any of my meetings with Dutch officials I will thoroughly research and familiarize myself with who this person is and what their accomplishments are. I am aware that Daan Vossem has been in his mayoral position since 1921 and he is a well-respected man. He is a man of integrity as he puts the needs of his city and residents first."

When I arrive at the Mayor's office, I give Herr Daan the Hitler salute (siegtteil salute) and yell "Heil Hitler."

Daan does not respond to my greeting. I stand still and glare at him hoping to make him feel uncomfortable. I can tell that I am making him feel uneasy as he cannot look me in the eye and his eyes are darting everywhere like shooting stars. He offers me a seat in one of his plush chairs, but I refuse. I have had enough disrespect from his weak man!

"Herr Vossem, you must realize by now that you are under MY command. I own your life and that of your family's. When I or any of my appointed officials enter your building, office, hallway, or lavatory you WILL salute each of us, and say "Heil Hitler."

Willem is trembling not from fear but anger.

I further insult this weakling, "Now, Daan Vossem, I want you to get off your ass and give me the proper Nazi greeting. NOW!"

Daan arises from his desk and walks over to me holding his head high. He glares at me with his emerald green eyes and promptly gives the proper Nazi salute and in a loud voice shouts, "Heil Hitler."

He says this with a smug look on his face but pretend I believe him. "Good Daan, you are a fast learner. "Heil Hitler."

I am not a stupid man and know that Daan is probably thinking of ways to kill me. He is smart enough to internalize his feelings about me and the Nazi Regime. The Netherlands are spiraling into deep dark times and in order to personally survive and fulfill his mayoral duties he has to appear that he supports the Nazi regime. I glance around his office and take note of the pathetic décor. There is a little Dutch flag perched on his desk, Queen Wilhelmina's stunning portrait is on his wall, and there is a bouquet of white carnations on his official meeting desk. I decide to stay quiet for the moment but make a mental note to force him to get rid of his Dutch patriotic symbols and have him replace them with the Nazi symbols.

Several days after my encounter with the Mayor of Amsterdam, I arrange a meeting with Joep Van Kaan, the infamous leader of the NSB. I am aware that Joep has previously met with Hitler in Berlin and that his goal is for an independent Netherlands. I am also aware that Adolf speaks abruptly to Joep and instructs him to focus on curtailing any disobedient Dutch resident's behaviors and not promoting an independent Netherlands.

In my meeting with Joep, I anoint him with the honorary title, "Leader of the Dutch People" (Leider va het Nederlandse Volk). In reality, Joep is not given any actual power; in fact, Herr Joep's power is controlling the unruly behaviors of the Dutch population. I also permit Joep and members of the NSB to continue carrying their NSB cards. These NSB identification cards contain a member's name, date of birth, membership card number and the date of issue. I am aware that these bright yellow cards with a black and red flag are powerful symbols for the NSB. Anyone who carries these can flash them to the Dutch populace as an extension of their power. I reinforce my commitment to Joep and the NSB provided they work diligently toward oppressing any resistance to the German occupation.

7

HELGA

At sixteen years of age, I was accepted into the languages program at the University of Amsterdam. In spite of my young age, I excel in both Germanic and Romantic Languages. While I am fluent in many languages, I am a still a little rusty with Italian. It is important to note that my university studies expand on the language and culturally rich experiences my parents nourished me with all my life.

Ever since I can remember, I have been bathed in different languages and cultural experiences. Our housekeeper, Olga is from St. Petersburg, Russia. As a young child she taught me Russian, enriched me with her experiences with Nikolai II, Alexandrovich Romanov (Tsar Nicholas II), his wife Alexandra Feodorovna (Alix of Hess), their children and the rise of communism. Her grandfather was a member of the Imperial Guard who protected the Russian royal family. She would elaborate on how, as a child she met the Royal Family and even became friends with Grand Duchess Anastasia Nikolaevna of Russia. She tells me of how weak and pale young Alexei Nikolaevich Tsarevich of Russia was. It is sad.

She tells me that after the execution of the Russian Royal Family, the Romanovs, the Communist Red soldiers hunted and executed any Whites and Supporters of Tsar Nicholas II. Olga could not recall the date, but one night her father did not come home, and her mother assumed that he was either hiding, captured, or executed by the Reds. Tears filled her eyes as she shared with me how she and her mother left most of their belongings and treasures in their St. Petersburg home and fled for their lives. They each carried a small bag with water, food, a few articles of clothing, and a few treasures they could keep or even use to barter for food or their lives. They hid in barns during the day and walked aimlessly through fields, forests, and tried to cross streams without getting wet at night in order to escape the vodka induced Reds.

One evening when they were both exhausted, they found an isolated farm and snuck into the barn. They found horses in their stalls and walked past these stalls to a pile of clean straw. Olga remembered how she tucked straw around her mother and gave her winter coat to her. Her mother protested but Olga whispered that she was fine as she was wearing many layers of clothes. Olga wanted to stay and protect her mother, but her mother pushed her away. Tears flowed from her eyes as she spoke about how her mother forced her to abandon her when her body was cooking from a high fever, her breathing labored, and her dangerously loud cough could at any time reveal their hiding spot to any Red within ear shot. Her mother told her to go, fight to survive, and tell their story to anyone who would listen. Her mother placed her wedding rings and her gold chain with her sacred Russian Orthodox Crucifix hanging off of it waving in the wind to defend the wearer against the devil in Olga's hands. They both said a prayer that the owners of the farm were not Communists. Then Olga and her mother both crying hard, hugged and exchanged kisses. She told her mother that she would head southwest to get out of Russia and that she would look for her when it was safe. The last time she saw her mother she was wrapped in a frayed horse blanket shivering and trying to muffle her deep bronchial cough. I can tell by the way that Olga is speaking and by her facial expressions that she is still consumed with guilt to this day. The memories of leaving her mother to succumb to her illness or at the hands of the vengeful Reds and promising her mother that she would look for her, were nightmares that Olga would never forget.

She shared with me her reoccurring haunting dream. She and her mother were running for their lives as they were being chased by vengeful Red soldiers. They were far enough ahead of them that they were able to hide and catch their breath by an outcrop in a thick stand of taiga trees. Her mother instructed her to take the Tokarev SVT-38 semi-automatic rifle and hide in the stand of taiga trees 25 meters from the outcrop. This stand of trees provided a perfect view for any incoming soldiers.

Olga said It seemed like forever before one of the soldiers found her mother. Before, he could confront her, Olga fired her rifle and he collapsed onto the ground. They were aware that the shot that was fired would be heard by the other soldiers and they would immediately run toward the shot gun blast. Her mother cautiously joined her at the stand of trees. The soldiers strategically arrived to find their dead comrade. Their military training had them on the defensive, but Olga and her mother were in survival mode. They waited until each of the soldiers was within sight and then Olga fired a volley of shots. Another one was dead. Where was the third one? She shifted her position within the protection of the trees. Ah, there he is the Red fool! One bullet and he was down. Olga said she looked at her mother and smiled. Not too bad for a woman who prefers making bread to firing a semi-automatic rifle.

Olga's told me her mother was shivering from the cold and the infection was consuming her body. She said she put her coat on her as she was wearing several sweaters and said, "Mother, we must find you shelter."

"Olga, you must leave me. Go in peace and survive. Olga, you are my glimmer of hope for the future."

At the end of the dream, she said her mother was standing strong with her infectious smile, sparkling teak blue eyes, and her strong arms. She was surrounded by men and women armed with rifles. The soldiers in the dream apparently looked more like rebels as they were not wearing the standard Communist soldier uniform. She extended her one arm with a semi-automatic rifle secured in her left hand; her other arm was reaching out to welcome Olga for a visit. Olga interprets this dream as her mother wanting her to participate in the fight for freedom.

Olga speaks boldly and matter of fact to me. "The Russians destroyed my family, my childhood, and continue to poison my dreams. But I am a fighter who has survived the horror of the Russian Revolution and I am prepared to fight the Nazis to the bitter end. I know that mother will guide me in my dreams and her Russian Orthodox cross will protect me from evil."

I give Olga a hug and I tell her that I will always protect her and Lukasz as they are both part of my family.

"I know Helga, I have lost one family and I will not lose another."

Deep down my heart aches for Olga and Lukasz. I am sure that he as a similar background. I pledge to protect my family, Olga, and Lukasz to the best of my ability. I look into Olga's face and I can see sorrow and tears in her eyes. I give her a big hug, tell her that I love her, and that we are a strong family, and the Nazis will not destroy us.

Every October 1, Olga has a special celebration with our family. With her permission my best friend Leike attends this annual celebration. Leike and I have been friends since we were six years of age. I believe that Olga has this annual celebration because she hopes to make a spiritual connection with her mother and father while enjoying this special time with her adoptive family and Leike. Olga is quite fond of Leike and refers to her as her other daughter! This celebration is the Feast of the Protection of the Theotokos or Intercession of the Theotokos and is always in the seclusion and security of our home. This feast is the revelation of Theotokos' protection which is spread over the world and the Mother of God's great love for mankind. Along with an exquisitely prepared Russian meal, all of us recite the following prayer: "Remember us in your prayers, O Lady Virgin Mother of God, that we not perish by the increase of our sins. Protect us from every evil and grievous woes, for in you do we hope, and venerating the Feast of your protection we magnify you."

Lukasz, on the other hand, is very guarded and secretive of his past. It is as if he descended on a cloud in the bright blue sky. It's a mystery. When I ask mother and father, they tell me not to quiz him on his past. All I know is that he is from Poland and does not have any family.

Yet, in spite of their tragic and unknown pasts, both Olga and Lukasz continue to educate me on their customs and their languages. When I was a child, I would say the Lord's Prayer in Russia one night, Polish the next, Dutch the next, etc. As a child I often wondered if I confused God by mixing up the languages and words. One night, I tested God by interchanging Russian and Polish words in the Lord's Prayer. I giggled out loud but then I felt embarrassed. I could feel my face turning beet red. I was not sure if that was due to my embarrassment or God getting even with me. I ran out of my bedroom and into Mother's arms.

"Mother, I hope God is not angry with me as I have tested him by mixing up my words in the Lord's Prayer." I giggle as I thought it is funny that I can fool God.

"Helga, God loves you for who you are. Go upstairs, get on your knees. Tell God that you are sorry for testing him and pray for his forgiveness. God will forgive you. Remember, God is the one who will test you!"

I remember this incident as if it were yesterday. The next day, I practiced the Lord's Prayer in the different languages and I made sure I said the words correctly from that night onward. I remember looking over my shoulder to see if God was following me to test me.

I praise my parents for exposing me to the 'world'. My dream is to go to New York City in America. Father wants me to follow in his footsteps and become a doctor. But to be honest, I hate the antiseptic smell of hospitals and the sight of blood makes my stomach churn. I devised a way to keep Father happy; he utilizes my language skills to translate when his patients do not understand Dutch as Father is unfamiliar with the foreign language. He comments that having someone speak in his or her native language can help reduce anxiety.

My parents are very proud of my achievements. They are famous for the lavish parties they host, and they constantly brag about my successes. These events attract politicians, military personnel, medical colleagues, and other elite members of Amsterdam society. This exposure paid off as I am a language tutor for several wealthy families, including the Mayor of Amsterdam. At these parties I dress in elegant evening wear. My favorite evening gown is one of mother's creation. It is made of black crepe georgette with natural-colored machine lace, long and slightly dragging, decorated with wrinkled strips of crepe georgette. It is a very conservative style and does not cling to my figure nor it as seductive as other gowns I have seen women wearing at these parties. I wear my long blond hair in a fringe roll, cascading to the middle of my back. Mother always dresses me classy for these events. Olga and Lukasz are also smartly dressed for these occasions and mother always assists in serving drinks, hors d'oeuvres, or wherever she can.

CHAPTER EIGHT

Leike is my best friend. Growing up we were always in the same class during our primary school years. Her family lived 30 minutes from my house in an older area of the city. When Leike was 14 her mother was killed in a car accident. It was a very difficult time for both her and her father. Her father took it extremely hard and had a difficult time coping with his wife's death. Leike, being an only child, became his caregiver. Her family was not prosperous so we assisted them as much as we could. Olga would prepare extra food and Father, or Lukasz would drop it off at their house. I know Leike was very embarrassed at this but to the best of my knowledge she wasn't insulted but thankful. Her father did not say much as he seemed to be lost in his own little world.

One year after losing her mother her father passed away, in his favorite chair with a bottle of vodka in his hand. Leike took the loss of both parents within a short period of time extremely hard. Father paid for his funeral. It was a small gathering as Leike kept to herself; I was her only true friend. Several days after his passing Leike telephoned me to help clean out her family home as she was moving. She kept some of her mother's china and jewelry. I offered to store any extra special items she would like to keep. Leike just mumbled and I let her do her own thing. I assigned myself cleaning duties, I swept, scrubbed, washed, and polished wood floors. I was Leike's shadow as whenever she finished sifting through the room's contents, I was there to thoroughly clean after her.

We completed the work in two days. I knew that it was taking a toll on her emotions as I could hear her crying. I tried many times to console her, but she insisted on being left alone. The first night, Leike agreed to stay at my house. I contacted Father and he picked us up, placed my bicycle in the trunk of his car and loaded several boxes of keepsakes for her.

Olga prepared a nice baked vegetable dish with homemade Dutch bread. The adults tried their best to make the dinner conversation light and airy. It didn't really work but at least they tried. Leike and I excused ourselves after gulping down the meal. I insisted that she take a bath and relax. I set out a night dress for her. I knew that she wanted to sleep beside me, but I didn't want to encourage her. I understood that she was hurting from the loss of her parents, but I did not want to be her sexual outlet. Leike was a lesbian and very fond of me. I told her many times that while I loved her as a friend, I did not want to have a relationship with her. I knew she was hurt by my comment, but I had to be straightforward as I did not want to lose a great loyal friend over any sexual encounter.

We slept in separate rooms and I fell asleep as soon as my head hit my pillow. It was Sunday and we slept in until 09:00. After a quick breakfast with tea, Olga handed me a basket with bread, cheese, and fruit for our lunch. What a sweetheart. Father drove us to Leike's place. She was more upbeat this morning. It is amazing what a good night sleep does for a mind and soul. She stated that she hasn't had such a good night's sleep in years.

Father drops us off and says he will pick us up around 16:00. That gives us ample time to finish our chores. Leike had saved some of her mother's dresses so she packs them up along with some linen for my mother. Mother can make a masterpiece out of rags! Leike keeps her mother's china cabinet and contents, her bed and her mother's inherited chest of drawers, and personal stuff such as family pictures, her school awards, and other important memorabilia. She tells her neighbor that she can have the left-over furniture and any of the items that are still useable.

I check on Leike during the day and she is in better spirits. I honestly think that she is seeing the light at the end of the tunnel. Father arrives and Leike instructs him to drop her and her personal items at her new address. We leave her trusted neighbor with the house key and tell her that the new owner of the house will pick it up from her in a few days. As we leave the house Leike's eyes begin to overflow with tears. I hug her as she says goodbye to her mother, father, and her life as she knew it. When we arrive at Leike's new home, Father and I help her carry her belongings into the sorting room – the living room. We meet Mrs. Van Der Steek the house owner and I whisper in her ear "Please take care of Leike. She is a little frail right now". After speaking those words to Mrs. V, I chuckle and scold myself as she is the frail older lady that should need looking after. Helga, I think to myself, you could have chosen your words better!

After thirty minutes we leave Leike and the ample leftovers in Olga's basket and say goodbye. Leike says she will contact me when she is ready. I agree as I know she has a lot to process as her life has drastically changed. I do not realize that this will be the last time I will see her for some time.

CHAPTER NINE

I n the back of my mind, I hope and pray that I can continue my private language tutoring. I have five students who are all at different levels in their foreign language training. I enjoy enriching my lessons by providing my students with cultural insights. But now with the Nazi occupation, I must be very careful with what I teach and to whom. I do not want the Nazis to accuse and subsequently charge me with promoting communism or supporting Jews.

I also think of Leike and wonder what she is doing with her life. I haven't seen her since she moved into Mrs. V's home. She clearly went into isolation. I hope and pray that she is safe and has found herself again.

On the evening of May 21, 1940, Mother, Father and I are residing in the parlor enjoying a cup of tea with Olga's famous Russian dessert baked varenye made with tart apples, sweet apples, and sugar. She cooks this dessert to perfection, and it is perfect with our tea. We are startled when we hear a knock on the door. Father gets up to answer it and to his surprise, standing in the doorway are the Mayor of Amsterdam, Mr. Vossem, and two SS officers that are perfectly dressed in their starched gray uniforms, ugly Nazi insignias, and polished black high boots. I can see our guests from the sofa in the parlor and my heart is racing. What have we done to deserve this meeting? Since, the Nazi invasion, I have become very paranoid. It is later at night and the moon has crept into our house through the open door, casting ominous shadows on our walls. The shadows on our walls remind me of monsters rising out of hell, our living hell which is Nazism.

"Lars, good evening, may I speak to Fraulein Helga?" Daan requests politely.

I can see that Father is quite taken aback by the Fraulein comment. To be honest, so am I. Mr. Vossem a Nazi! I would never have imagined him turning to the dark side of humanity.

"Yes, Daan one moment please."

Overhearing the conversation between Father and Mr. Vossem, I slowly walk into the foyer.

"Good evening Mr. Vossem."

"Good evening Fraulein Helga."

When he calls me Fraulein Helga I must give him a look of surprise because he gives me a quick smile and a wink.

"Fraulein, your language skills and reputation are impeccable. Your skills are very valuable to the Third Reich. We want to utilize your skills at the Amsterdam Central Registry. You will assist individuals updating their census and identification cards. I expect you to report to Herr Doff Boumer, the Registry manager, tomorrow at 08:00 sharp. As you are aware the Registry's address is Plantage Kerlaan 36-38.

"I am through listening to this garbage!" I think to myself.

"Mr. Vossem, do you expect me to support the Nazi occupiers? I will NEVER support a regime that invades a country and murders innocent civilians!"

Where has the kind Mr. Vossem gone; did they transform him into a Nazi monster? Mr. Vossem gives me a stern look and I know that he is not pleased with my response.

"Fraulein Helga, this is a command, and it will not be negotiated! This is not an option but an ORDER THAT YOU WILL OBEY OR SUFFER SEVERE CONSEQUENCES!"

Father invades the conversation with a stern disrespectful voice. "Daan, are you trying to intimidate my daughter? We have known each other professionally and privately for years. What is the matter with you? I will not tolerate your attitude."

"Herr Lars, these are different times, I arrive at your doorstep as a sign of respect for you and your family. Ared Schwarz could have sent the SS officers or a Gestapo agent to instruct Helga of her appointment. I know that they are not as cordial as I am. Fraulein Helga, we expect you at the Registry at 08:00 SHARP. Just in case you and your family did not adjust your clocks to the implemented German time, or you forget or sleep in, I will have these two SS officers escort you into the Central Registry building. This matter is now closed! Goodbye."

Mr. Vossom turns to face us before he exits through the open door. He has an apologetic look on his face. He raises his arm, in the Hitler salute, and shouts "Heil Hitler". His final comment to us is "Get used to the new way of life!"

Once he leaves, we all look at each other in disbelief.

"Father, they can't do this to me or us!"

Mother is her usual self, adding fuel to an already extremely volatile situation. She is frantic and babbling nonsense flows from her like an overflowing stream drowning anything in its path.

"*Fuck, I don't need this now.*" I think to myself. I am not in the mood to hear her squawking like a parrot.

I excuse myself and go to my bedroom. I leave Father to perform his magic on Mother and calm her down. I cannot overhear what is being said but I am sure that Father is reassuring her that I am a smart analytical woman, and I will be fine. I am sure he has to stress several times that I can take care of myself! Most of the time Father gives Mother half or a full sedative to calm her down.

I don't sleep well as my mind keeps playing scenarios over and over about the Nazi occupation. Olga wakes me up and I drag myself out of bed and take a quick bath. I tie my hair back and put on a fitted knee length plain red dress and stockings with seams in the back. Mother gives me her favorite navy-blue scarf to finish my look. I eat my breakfast very slowly as my stomach is in knots. I feel l could vomit, but I don't. I try to engage in pleasantries with my family. Father joins Mother, Lukasz, Olga, and I for breakfast. He insists on being at home when my escort arrives. I may be a grown woman, but I am still a little girl in his eyes.

Father speaks to me away from Mother's prying ears. "Helga, they will be watching you. You must be careful and perform your tasks diligently. Remember, there are spies everywhere."

"Yes Father, I know, and I will be careful."

Mother's eyes are full of tears. I reinforce with her that I will be fine and not to worry. I tell her I will be home for dinner tonight. She is not as frantic as she was last night. I assume that a good night's rest and an evening sedative did their magic. I give everyone hugs and tell them that I will be fine and home for dinner.

CHAPTER TEN

My escorts arrive at 07:30 sharp with loud repetitive knocks on our door. I say good morning to them, but the SS officers don't say a word. They escort me out our front door, down our sidewalk and to the awaiting sedan complete with a uniformed driver. One soldier opens the right rear sedan door for me and I politely accept his gesture. The other soldier opens the left side door and sits beside me. Great, a rose between two thorns! The ride is silent except for my racing heart. I look down at my dress to see if the rapid beating can be seen or heard outside my body. Nothing is visible to the naked eye. I glare at both of my escorts and their faces are expressionless and cold like the tip of an iceberg protecting the layers beneath the ocean. We arrive at the Registry and they escort me up the stairs where I am greeted by Mr. Vossem and Doff Boumer, who I assume is the Registry Manager.

"Good morning, Fraulein Helga, I hope you slept well?" Mr. Vossem says in a concerned voice.

I look at him and see he is dressed in a charcoal suit complete with a red tie and penny loafers. Mr. Boumer is very sharply dressed in a tailored navy-blue pin stripe suit and a matching double-breasted jacket with wide peak lapels and welled chest pocket. His perfectly pressed dress shirt is cream with French cuffs and one pocket. His wide tie is red with navy blue curly lines. I look down at his feet and notice he is wearing black leather shoes. He has an enticing male scent. His tailored outfit suits his dark brown hair, teal blue eyes, and smooth skin. He is very handsome but unfortunately, he supports the Nazi Regime.

I had planned to snap at each one of them, but Father, Olga and Lukasz instructed me to be quiet and not make any waves. They all know that if I want to, I can create a tsunami when I'm angry! They all know I'm extremely angry at thought of helping the Nazis.

"Yes, I slept fine thank you and I am looking forward to working at the Registry."

Mr. Vossem raises his eyebrows, winks at me. "Great, I am glad you have come to your senses."

I know that Mr. Vossem understands my sarcasm but I'm not too sure about Doff Boumer. Mr. Vossem stays for the introduction and then excuses himself and leaves.

The first thing Mr. Boumer does is lead me into his office. I feel many sets of eyes piercing my body as I walk past the maze of workers. I wonder if these women are willingly supporting the Third Reich or, are they being forced into it like me? I know that in time, I will investigate each and every one of my colleagues; I will weed out the Nazi supporters. After we enter his office, he closes his door.

"Fraulein Helga, I want to speak to you privately without worrying about nosey women hearing us."

"Herr Boumer, I understand."

A well-dressed older woman with graying hair that is pulled back in a bun, and has makeup caked on so heavy she must have to chisel it off every night, enters carrying a tea tray complete with a plate of mixed German cookies. Olga has made me these same kind of cookies before and I know they are delicious. After she sets the tray down on the ornate teak meeting table she leaves with a slight bow of her head. Mr. Boumer invites me to sit down at the table and after sitting I take a moment to look around. The back wall is lined with a beautiful intricate detailed mahogany bookcase housing German and Dutch books. Beside the bookcase there are two 4 drawer filing cabinets, each with files and papers neatly stacked on each of them. His desk is another teak masterpiece. On top of it, on the side, is a pencil holder with an array of writing utensils and an ink well with a beautiful pen lying beside it. There is a framed picture of a young woman strategically set in the middle of his desk. I wonder to myself if it is his wife or lover? On the right side of his desk is a Nazi flag standing erect in its base. I search his walls for any evidence that we are in the Netherlands. Nowhere in the office is a portrait of the Queen or the Netherlands flag. Overlooking the office is a large portrait of Adolf Hitler; he is perched high above us as if to remind us of who is in charge.

"Fraulein Helga, I am sure that you have personal experience with the Registry?"

"Yes, I have as I updated my census card when it is required."

"Yes, I know. I have it here actually. You will need to update it again as you are now working here."

"Yes, Herr Boumer, I understand."

"Fraulein, the Nazis are very thorough in their records. They want to have strict control over all citizens and residents, especially the Jews, Roma, homosexuals, communists, and other undesirable groups. These individuals are not worthy of life according to the Third Reich."

I cannot believe what he is spewing out of his mouth! I can't believe I am going to be part of this sick doctrine which is straight out of the pages of Mein Kompf.

"Fraulein Helga, in case you are wondering, the Gestapo investigated your family before you were selected for this position. Your father is a doctor and your mother an accomplished dressmaker. Your servants Olga and Lukasz have raised red flags; but we will deal with them later. Right now, our focus is to utilize your language skills to make people feel at ease when they are updating their census cards and getting their identification cards. It is a psychological move by the Reich as people will be more at ease speaking with a well-respected Dutch woman than a German woman. Am I correct that you speak Jew?"

I look at him in disgust and sternly respond, "If you are referring to Yiddish, yes sir, I am fluent in speaking and writing this ancient language."

"Great, this will put the Jewish filth at ease when they infect our registry."

At this point, I quit focusing on his words. His Jew comment was disgusting but I am more concerned about the comment he made that Olga and Lukasz will be dealt with later. These words are saturating my mind. What does he mean by deal with them later? I must warn them. I must protect my beloved family. I have completely tuned out what he is saying and am startled when he abruptly slaps the table to bring me back to the present.

"Fraulein, as I was asking several times, do you have your passport with you?"

"No sir, I didn't realize that I required it."

"Fraulein, today I will personally see to it that you get an identification card. You will need it to enter this building and in case you are stopped by Nazi soldiers or the NSB. I will instruct one of our photographers to take your picture today so you can get your identification card before you leave work today. You must understand that this is very important work entrusted to us by the Nazis. The Nazis have non-uniformed SS officers in the registry overseeing our work."

Great, I will have Nazi filth hovering around!

"Let's go out into the production area where I will introduce you to your colleagues and show you where everything is kept." His frumpy secretary sits to the right of his office. She has her own three drawer filing cabinet nestled in the corner behind her desk. This cabinet must contain confidential documents as it is the locking kind and there is a key chain dangling from the lock. Ten three-drawer filing cabinets are lined up against the walls forming a perimeter in the production area. In the center are seven desks with typewriters. We walk the perimeter of the room as he briefly tells me where the blank census cards, blank identification cards, and completed cards are housed. He explains to me that all of the cabinets are locked at night and the keys are given to him.

I ask him about the closed door that is across from his office, yet strategically placed away from my colleague's desks. Doff informs me that this room is off limits. We walk over to a vacant desk in the maze of desks and he tells me that this will be mine. I set my purse and jacket on it and we continue the tour.

Next, I am formally introduced to my colleagues. My desk is located between Leos, a middle-aged petite Dutch woman, and Eva, a young voluptuous Nazi. Lucky me, I am positioned between the oppressor and the oppressed. As Doff introduces me to my other colleagues I try to discern their accents. I am working with two Dutch woman and four Nazis. The women are polite but standoffish. I don't blame them. I am new blood invading their little empire; I know they will test me. But I will also test each and every one of them in return. The production area is infested with Nazi propaganda. Every desk is poisoned by a small erect Nazi flag and positioned high above the production area is another portrait of Hitler overlooking his servants.

Once the brief introduction is completed, Doff ushes me back into his office. As he pours us a cup of tea, he stresses that it is important that I understand the identification process.

"The Nazis are competent in their record keeping and they expect us to be as thorough and diligent. First, an individual will complete a census card; this card will contain the person's full name, date of birth, age, address, occupation, religion, etc. From this information you will create an identification card that contains the same information. These identification cards are of superior quality and cannot be forged. Each card is made of three layers of different paper and different water marks. They are laminated together with a photograph and fingerprint inserted within the layers. The number on the identification card is recorded on the census card. The identification card is required for ration cards and must be carried at all times. If by chance a card is altered or lost and claimed by another person it will be useless because the Nazis can crosscheck information here and at the main registry in Berlin. Any individual caught forging or assisting in the alteration of these cards will be apprehended by the Gestapo. The Gestapo are ruthless and they will interrogate and torture the person or persons involved in the process. They do not take this form of terrorism lightly. In a rare occasion a person may be released, but most likely anyone involved with terrorism against the Third Reich will be sent to our police prison in Amsterdam or to a German prison. Fraulein Helga, I hope you understand the seriousness of our actions. I am a Dutchman who is responsible for my employee's actions. I am held accountable for you and the other employees' actions. If one of you are suspected of engaging in terrorist activities, I will also be interrogated by the Gestapo! Do you understand Fraulein Helga?"

"Yes, I do Herr Boumer!"

"Good girl, we will get along great," he says with a twinkle in his Nazi loving teal blue eyes.

"Now, Fraulein Helga, I will entrust you to Leos. She will work with you at the front counter and teach you how to competently complete these cards."

As we leave his office, his secretary, Mrs. Van Der Wert immediately retrieves our leftover snacks and sets them out for the ladies.

The front reception area contains a pine counter which is approximately four meters long and it can easily accommodate three employees assisting individuals and their families. The finish is bare in places and the wood is riddled with scratches and welts. The ancient pine knots are filled with ink and holes. Ah, this is where the frustrated individuals take out their anger. On the left side of the desk is a Dutch flag standing erect on its base. The left side also has writing utensils and an ink pad for fingerprints. There is one old chair against the wall facing the counter.

The walls are a drab olive green in color with a distinct faded square above the counter. I bet that was where the Queen's portrait resided until the occupation. At least we don't have Adolf overshadowing us. Under the counter are all of our supplies: an extra fingerprint ink pad, a container of extra ink, census cards, identification cards and blank pieces of paper. The laminating machine is located on a desk behind us so we can easily complete identification cards.

There is already a lineup of people impatiently waiting for Leos and me to assist them. I try to appease the waiting people by explaining that I am new to this position and ask them to please be patient. I catch a few eyes rolling but I will get over it. I know they don't care what I am saying, all they want is to get their identification cards processed and get the hell out of the office. The first lady that Leos and I assist is a middle-aged Dutch woman who is updating her census card and wants to get her official identification card. This lady is changing her address. I retrieve her census card from the back cabinet and update the card in duplicate. She did not bring in a recent photograph so I cannot give her new identification card to her. In spite of being annoyed, the lady is polite and thanks me for helping her.

After lunch, I am taken to the Centre's preferred photographer and smile for the camera. Leo assists me with updating my census card in duplicate and completing my identification card. The photographer arrives with my picture shortly after I visit him. I am fingerprinted and my identification card number is recorded on my census card. I place both my census card and the Dutch lady's I assisted earlier on top of the designated filing cabinet. Throughout the day I watch as the duplicate cards disappear into the secret Nazi abyss. I must find out what they are doing with these cards. I bet that it is not ethical and is most likely advancing the Nazis' control on us!

The day is long and gut wrenching. All I can think of is Olga and Lukasz and what is in store for them. At the end of the day, Herr Boumer offers to give me a ride home and I accept his offer.

Oh shit, he will know where I live. Relax Helga, he knows all about you!

He did not ask me for my address and like Nazi magic he delivers me to my house. I thank him and inform him that from tomorrow onward, I will ride my bicycle to work. He opens my door for me. I thank him again and scurry up my sidewalk into my sanctuary.

Once I enter the door to my sanctuary, I am inundated with a non-stop stream of questions asking me about my day at the Registry. I excuse myself and immediately collapse on our sofa. Olga instinctively brings me a glass of Taittinger Brut La Francaise Champagne and a little plate of dark chocolate. Father is at work and I know that Mother is not mentally prepared for what I have learned today. I tell Mother that I assisted a nice Dutch woman with her census card and one of my colleagues is a nice Dutch lady whose name is Leos. I feed her enough information to satisfy her concern and curiosity.

In contrast, I tell Olga to grab Lukasz and I inform them about the process, the secret room, and the comments Boumer made about them. I expect both of them to be shocked at my findings, but they take it all in stride. I comment that dark times are coming and we must prepare a hiding place for them. I will discuss this with Father. We all agree. Now I relax and savor my father's champagne and bitter chocolate.

We have a wonderful chicken and vegetable dinner prepared by Olga. Father is working late and though I am tired I must speak to him. To keep Mother happy, I kiss her goodnight and go to bed. I do not go to sleep though, as I am waiting to hear Father's key in the front door.

Around 02:00 Father arrives home from the hospital. I come

downstairs as he is eating his dinner cold. I tell him about my day and my concerns for Olga and Lukasz. He agrees that we need to modify the inside of our house to include safe rooms. He says he will talk to Lukasz about building these rooms for us. I give him a hug and a kiss goodnight before heading back upstairs. I quickly fall asleep, confident that we will take care of Olga and Lukasz.

CHAPTER ELEVEN

As the hours turn into days and days into weeks, I become more confident in my work at the registry. My work is still thoroughly scrutinized and a civilian dressed SS officer hovers over me like a hawk waiting for an opportunity to devour its prey. My colleagues are beginning to warm up to me and Leos and I are becoming good friends. I hope that one day soon Boumer will be confident with my work. I really want to get into the secret room and find out what the Germans are hiding.

Every morning we have a short pre-work meeting where Boumer updates us of any events that will impact our work. Today the Nazis announce that they want a complete census of all residents and inhabitants of Amsterdam. I am disturbed with this announcement as I know the Nazis are doing something secretly with this information.

Today, a well-dressed man with a crappy Dutch accent comes into the Registry to update his personal information on his census and identification cards. I sense that this could be a test as the man has a Dutch name and is speaking with a thick German accent. When I look at his identification card I see many inconsistences. When I analyze his card, it is clear that the three layers have been pried open and somehow reconnected. Also, his signature looks like it has been altered. I grab a blank piece of paper and ask him to write his signature on this paper for me. At first, he is reluctant but when I threaten to get Herr Boumer and the SS officers to assist me with my request, he quickly scribbles his signature on the paper. Just as I thought. As I look at the scribbled mess of his signature I can clearly see they do not match. I eye him up and down, he reminds me of a well-dressed Gestapo agent. I immediately alert two SS men who are standing nearby and tell them there is an issue. I quickly explain what is going on and they grab him as he tries to get away. They haul him up the stairs by his arms, roughing him up as they lead him to Boumer's office. I follow behind with the documents in my hands. I leave a frightened Leos to tend to the startled individuals in the long line up. I close the door in Mr. Boumer's office and direct everyone's attention to the inconsistencies in his signature and his pathetic attempt to tamper with the card. I also point out that he did a piss poor job of mimicking a Dutch national with his German accent.

I decide to stand up for myself.

"This man has clearly tampered with his identification; he is a terrorist and must be handed over to the Gestapo for interrogation."

Boumer, the two SS officers, and the forger look at me stunned before slowly smiling at me. The SS officers release the forger from their grip; then he turns to me and gives me an eerie evil smile.

"Fraulein Helga, very well done. You have succeeded in preventing a fraudulent identification card from distorting our identification system," remarks Herr Boumer. "You have done an excellent job at detecting a forged card. The Third Reich thanks you. As you are probably aware, this forger is actually a Gestapo agent."

"Fraulein Helga, I am impressed on how well you handled my situation," the Gestapo says.

Glaring at the men in front of me I exclaim, "I am so pleased that I passed your test. I hope now that I have proven my worth to the Third Reich and that the constant surveillance and tests are complete. Let me do my job in peace!"

I glare at Boumer and yell at him. "I am done! Excuse me as I go for a walk before I say something I shouldn't."

I slam the door behind me and several of my colleagues jump at the slam. Boumer comes out of the Nazi infested office and approaches me.

"Fraulein Helga, relax. We are happy with your work."

"Fine!" I sarcastically respond.

I collect my thoughts, take a deep breath, and go out to my position at the counter. I signal to Leos that I am alright. The day drags on and all I want to do is get the hell away from this place.

My bicycle ride home is very wobbly as I am shaking with anger and fear. Have my smart-ass comments gotten me in trouble with the Nazis? Did I trigger a tsunami? Have I put my mother, my father, Lukasz and Olga, in danger?

When I storm through the front door, Olga runs to me and asks me what is the matter. I tell her about the events of the day. Before she can respond, Mother darts out of her dressmaking room and asks what the commotion is all about?

"It was a very busy day at work," I tell her, walking away before she can quiz me further. It doesn't work as she follows me like a long-lost puppy.

"Helga, is there something you aren't telling me?"

"No, Mother everything is fine. We were just very busy at the registry today and had to turn many people away because they didn't have a current photograph. I wish the Germans would make an announcement on the radio and in the newspaper to remind people to bring a recent photograph. That is all Mother. Have you completed the mayor's wife's dress?"

"Helga, she is coming over tomorrow night for the final fitting. I will have the dress completed within a couple of days after that. It is going to be very beautiful. I will let you try it on, in secret of course."

Although Mother can be very annoying, I still love playing dress up even as a grown woman.

"Thank you, Mother. I look forward to it." I give her a hug and tell her that I love her.

"Love you also Helga." My mother says as she disappears back into little sanctuary.

Olga ushers me to the teak sofa while she boils water for Mother's tea and pours me a glass of Chardonnay before dinner. Olga delivers Mother's tea to her and I am relieved when she doesn't follow Olga out. Olga joins me on our sofa and I update her on the day's events.

"Helga, they are testing your loyalty to the Reich. You have successfully passed the test. Now you must be patient and see what is instore for you now at the registry. I believe that your boss will give you access to the secret room very soon."

"Olga, thank you for your kind words. I want to know what the Nazis are up to. Even my colleague Leos is at a loss as to what the Nazi fuckers are up to."

"Helga be careful and trust nobody. Be very observant and cautious at the registry. There are spies everywhere."

"Yes, Olga, I know, and I will. May I help you with dinner? Let me get changed out of these fancy clothes first."

"Oh, Helga," Olga yells up the stairs to me. "Your father will be home for dinner tonight."

I am very excited that Father is joining us for dinner. He is very busy at the hospital these days. He never elaborates on his work, but I am sure many of his patients have received beatings from the Germans and our NSB. I have to tell him my experience with the Gestapo at work.

The next couple hours fly by as Olga keeps me busy in the kitchen. I go out to our garden to harvest onions, carrots, and beets for dinner. I hear Lukasz pounding his hammer from the cellar. I am happy that he is diligently working on the safe rooms. I enjoy helping Olga prepare our meals and set the dining room table. To my family it is a special celebration when we are all at home for dinner. Olga and I both sip wine while we work. Olga is an amazing cook, and she feels more like my mom to me than my mother does.

Father arrives home a few minutes after 19:00 hours. He looks tired so I pour him a glass of chardonnay before dinner. I do not want to bombard him with my woes until we have finished dinner. The atmosphere during dinner is pleasant and quiet. I look around our dining room table and everyone looks tired, me included.

After dinner, Father and I retire to the parlor while Mother heads to her dressmaking room to get Mrs. Vossem's dress ready for the final fitting. I explain to Father what happened today at the registry. I am about to blurt out more words, but father hushes me when he puts his index finger to my mouth signaling me to be quiet and put on my listening ears.

"Helga, these are dangerous times. The Nazis are testing you and you must do what is required to survive. It sounds like you passed your unorthodox test. Please be our eyes and ears and keep us informed of what is going on. Sooner or later your boss will let something slip. Please be very observant at the registry and let us know what is going on. It is your responsibility to turn a negative situation into something positive."

"Father, you want me to be a spy?"

"Yes Helga, for our family. I want everyone to be safe."

Father is correct as I need to protect my family and Leike.

"Helga, I will talk with Lukasz when everyone has gone to sleep and see how he is progressing on the hiding spots."

I give him a big hug and kiss and I exit to my inner sanctuary - my bedroom. Here, in the silence and familiar surroundings I can think clearly and try to figure out a plan of attack for my new spy role.

CHAPTER TWELVE

I bike to work with my senses acutely aware of the surroundings. On my usual bike route, I come across a flower garden that I must have passed many times in my travels. I stop to look at this once beautiful, manicured garden which is now overrun with weeds and grasses. It is interesting that the weeds and grasses are thriving amongst the dried-up flowers. Have the flowers given up? The death and destruction in the flowerbed remind me of the current state of our country. Out of the corner of my eye, I see a lone resilient flower that is slightly risen above the chocking grasses and weeds. The stem is skinny and three small leaves look like they are trying to survive in the harsh garden conditions. This lone soldier reminds me of myself trying to survive the suffocating Nazis. But, in reality, this lone flower will also be decimated without the proper intervention. I get off my bike and clear several handfuls of weeds and grasses that are attempting to choke out the flower. Hopefully, I have given it a fighting chance. Goodbye my friend. I climb back on my bike to continue my ride to work. I know I will be late, but that lone flower needed my assistance. Did I help a resilient flower survive the oppression that is trying to destroy its existence?

I arrive at work a few minutes late. My hair must look like I went through a windstorm. Actually, riding my bicycle so fast had the exact same effect. I go into the lavatory to rearrange the tight ring-curls and waves that frame my face. I look at my reflection. I no longer see the weak defenseless woman I was, instead I see a lone flower thriving in the chaos of weeds and grasses.

As I leave the lavatory, Herr Boumer summons me to his office. To my surprise one of the SS officers who was part of the forgery incident is standing by the meeting table. I expect I am about to be reprimanded for my previous day's actions; instead, I see a tray of assorted chocolate and a bottle of Clio champagne on the table.

"Good gosh!" I say to myself, *"The Nazis also know about my love of champagne."*

""What is this?" I ask inquisitively.

"Fraulein Helga, the Reich would like to thank you for protecting our registry from the rebels. You have proven yourself to be a very worthy loyal member."

"Well sir, like I said yesterday, I was just doing my job," I boldly state.

"Fraulein, I understand that you were frustrated at our deceit. It is very important for me and the Nazis to know that you a trustworthy and loyal employee."

I look at him and I give him an apologetic smile. I expect Boumer and/or the SS office to keep yapping at me. Instead Boumer pours all three of us a glass of champagne and our toast is "Heil Hitler. We all respond with "Heil Hitler" and take a sip of the champagne. My mouth tingles as the bubbles dance in my mouth and my nose fills with the aromas of apple and pear while my palate is extra-dry with these amazing flavors. Even though it is before 09:00, I savor these bubbles that are teasing my mouth. To pair this champagne with chocolate is magnificent. I close my eyes savoring these flavors, hoping to be transported to a different place. I open my eyes and no such luck. I look out of the corner of my eye and see Herr Boumer is watching me savoring my morning treats. I look over at him and smile. I know that his special treatment will not be favorable with my colleagues. I sense that most of my colleagues still distrust me. I need to earn their trust. If I can do that with morning champagne and chocolate... it is worth a try.

"Excuse me gentlemen, but I believe that all of my colleagues should be able to enjoy these chocolates and a glass of champagne with us. This can hopefully soften any animosity they may have against me, Herr Boumer, and the Reich."

Boumer agrees and the SS officer leaves with a handful of chocolates. Boumer opens the door and invites my colleagues into his office to share the treats. As I stand by my desk in the back office, I watch as a procession of Dutch and German Nazis parade into Herr Boumer's office to express their gratitude to Hitler. Not one colleague refuses the offer. I am surprised at Leos, my Dutch colleague, who joins the line of little Nazis.

I cover the front counter for Leos and there is another long line of distressed people. I help several Jewish families who have been forced from their homes and now reside with relatives in cramped quarters. I speak to these people empathetically and in Yiddish. I recognize several faces as I was unable to process their identification cards prior due to them not having a recent photo with them the last time they came. The Jewish families I have assisted leave the registry with their questions answered and their identification cards in their hands. As like most days at the registry we are busy. As I assist the various families, I notice that many Jewish men and woman have died from heart issues according to family records. How can a twenty-five-year-old woman die of heart issues? Maybe if she has a history of heart issues and the Nazis have stolen all the medicine. I don't know, but I will ask Father what the hell is going one.

After assisting a Dutch lady with her cards, I look up at the next person and see that it is Leike. I run through the door that connects the front counter to the informal waiting area and give her a big hug and ask how she is doing. She looks great, a little thin, but that's all right. I hear grumblings from the long line of people so quickly hug her again and go back to work. She is here to update her census and identification cards. I retrieve her census card and am happy she did not put lesbian on the card. That is a no to the Nazis. We chat as I complete her paperwork. She tells me she completed her arts degree in calligraphy and photography at the University of Amsterdam. I am thrilled to hear this as I know both are her callings. She tells me she is still at Mrs. V's place and insists that I join the two of them for dinner. I agree as I all I have to do is telephone Olga and tell her not to prepare dinner for me.

When Leos returns to the front counter, she informs me that Herr

Boumer wants to speak to me. The tone in her voice indicates that she has no respect for him. Before I leave, she grabs my arm and whispers in my ear, "I had to line up like a good little Nazi or else they would suspect something is up with me."

I turn and look into her eyes and know exactly what she is implying. I smile and wink at her and go to Boumer's office.

"Herr Boumer, you wanted to speak to me?"

He closes his office door and looks at me seductively. "Helga your hair looks beautiful today."

"Herr Boumer, thank you. I never thought you noticed me." I teasingly reply.

"Yes, Helga I notice everything about you."

He walks up to me and gently kisses me on my right cheek. "You are very beautiful."

I lightly laugh and comment that he is a married man. He just smiles and puts his arm around my waist. He attempts to kiss my lips but I turn my head and he brushes my cheek.

"Herr Boumer, what will the Nazis think? What about your wife?" I look down at the massive bulge in the front of his pants.

"Beautiful Helga, see what you do to me?" He touches the bulge in the front of his pants. Then he looks into my robin's egg blue eyes that twinkle in the light from his office. To further entice him, I look into his eyes and give him a passionate kiss on his lips as my tongue investigates the inside of his mouth. When I am finished, I can see lust in his eyes.

"Herr Boumer, we must be careful as not to attract attention." I gently touch the mass in the front of his pants. "I apologize for my unladylike behavior."

"My lovely Helga, if you ever want anything please let me know."

Mmm good to know." I think to myself. *"I have him right where I want him."*

"Herr Boumer, can I please take the unfinished bottle of Clio with me tonight. I would hate it to go to waste." I pray that he does not insist that I finish it with him.

He nods his head and whispers that he will give me another bottle before I leave. I thank him and raise my arm in the Hitler salute and yell "Heil Hitler"! I realize now that I can take advantage of him and manipulate him like a blob of clay ready to be molded into a functionable piece of dinner ware.

Leos and I are busy with census and identification cards the remainder of the day. The day cannot end fast enough, I am so excited to see my friend after all this time. I tell Leos that I am going to visit my friend and am startled when she tells me to be careful. What is she talking about? Leike would never betray her friend or her country.

Before I leave for the day, I slip into Boumer's office to grab the bottles of Cleo he set aside for me. He is busy on the telephone and I thank God we can't speak. I blow him a kiss and off I go, closing the door behind me. I wrap my purse and bottles of champagne tightly in my sweater and place the bundle in my bicycle carrier. I don't want to be riding my bike with alcohol visible in my carrier. Those NSB and Nazi goons will for sure confiscate the bottles for themselves if they see them.

CHAPTER THIRTEEN

The bicycle ride to Leike's residence does not take me long. As I walk my bicycle up her sidewalk, I see her peeking out from under the blackout curtains. I set my bike by the side of the house and enter the unlocked door. I walk into the foyer and close the door behind me. She greets me with a big hug. My goodness she is beautiful with her ash blond curls, porcelain skin, emerald green eyes, and curvy body. *"Thank gosh I am not a lesbian or that woman would be mine,"* I think to myself.

"Darling, I have missed you." I say sincerely.

"I've missed you also."

"Leike, I have brought us some Clio champagne!"

As Leike retrieves the champagne flutes, I tell her about the events of the last couple days. I tell her about Boumer and the kisses and his throbbing erection. Her eyes are like saucers as she stares in disbelief.

"Leike, fucking German men, they think that can do what they want to us Dutch ladies."

"I would have stabbed him with a pencil!"

Wow, Leike has become aggressive.

As we sit on Mrs. V's couch, Leike informs me that she and a school colleague Ani have a small photography and calligraphy shop. Their business is very busy. Unbeknownst to me Mother has hired Leike's company in the past to create beautiful calligraphy invitations for her parties.

"My gosh Leike, I wish you or others had told me. I would have asked you to attend some of her lavish parties so you could get business referrals."

"Helga, your mother has been very good to me as she has referred many of her wealthy friends and clients to my business. Please tell your mother hello and thank her again for the referrals. Word gets around and now a lot of my work includes swastikas."

We both laugh.

I hear creaks on the stairs and see Mrs. V. is slowly descending the narrow stairs from the upper floor in her house. Leike grabs me by the arm and leans over to whisper, "I like to make sure that she does not slip and fall down the stairs. It annoys the hell out of her, but I tell her it is my job."

Mrs. V. is wearing her favorite slippers and grasping the bannister so she doesn't fall. We watch her come down the stairs, both of us anticipating a fall. But she fools us both.

Instead, she looks at me and says, "Miss Helga, don't stand there staring at me. Please bring me my cane and pour me a glass of that champagne I heard you and Leike speaking about."

I look at her with a smile on my face and give her a wink.

"Miss Helga, the walls are paper thin."

As Leike sets Mrs. V.'s favorite frayed mauve cushion into her special chair, I pour her a flute of Clio and deliver it to her as Leike adjusts her back cushion.

"My gosh Mrs. V. has incredible hearing for an old lady! I will have to keep that in mind!" I think to myself.

I apologize to both Leike and Mrs. V. that I did not bring any food. They both tell me not to worry as Leike is connected in the black market and they utilize both of their ration cards.

Her relaxation room, as she calls it, is connected to the kitchen. Her furniture is dated from the 1920's. Leike quietly tells me that when Mrs. V.'s husband died in early 1920, she decided to leave the house the way he liked it. Her gramophone sits in the corner of her relaxing room and I am sure it hasn't been played in decades. The interior of the house is a faded gray cream color. I see Leike's mother's cabinet with the amazing collection of china, crystal, and other pieces collected over the years placed opposite the couch and Mrs. V.'s favorite chair. To me it brings life to Mrs. V.'s relaxing room. The kitchen has a standalone sink and a freestanding cupboard. There is a small pantry where Leike stores dry goods like flour and sugar. What amazes me the most is the ancient wood burning cooking stove. Mrs. V. refuses to update it so Leike has become quite the expert cooking on her stove. Even the icebox is small and dated. The weekly ice man has modified his blocks of ice to fit it.

We talk about the Nazi occupation, the regular beatings we have witnessed, food rations, and the need to prepare for more restrictions. Leike surprises me when she mentions the underground newspapers and the increase in the number of Dutch individuals getting tired of all this Nazi crap. I don't say a word but Mrs. V. warns Leike to be quiet and not to speak ill of the Nazis as it is dangerous. Leike does not say a word.

Leike had taken the afternoon off work and paid a visit to her contacts and scrounged food for our dinner. I help set the table and pour Mrs. V. another flute of champagne. She joins us and insists on saying grace. She talks continuously during our meal of cooked potatoes, carrots, onions and fresh Dutch bread. She keeps repeating that she is delighted to have dinner with her two girls. But Mrs. V also has a serious side to her.

During dinner Mrs. V. pipes up, "Helga, you are a very smart woman. I understand you are working at the registry. It is important for you to keep yourself safe by being in the Nazis and their puppets' good books. Please be careful as they can turn on you like a rabid dog. Remember that they document and remember everything about everyone."

"Mrs. V., please don't worry, I will be careful. Thank you for your concern. You must be careful as well. Hitler is revered as the new god. I know you are a strong Christian lady, but please be careful who you talk to about your faith. The Nazis don't like that and you can get yourself into serious trouble."

"Dear Helga, I know these are dangerous times. I will not give up my Christian faith for the Third Reich. They can throw me in jail if they want, but I know that I am protected."

Leike and I smile and agree with her. Leike retrieves her baked apples from the oven. The smell of sweet baked apples with cinnamon permeates the air. Everything becomes quiet as we savor Leike's dessert.

After tidying up the dishes, Mrs. V. has another flute of champagne and then asks Leike to help her up the stairs to her bedroom. She has had a lot of champagne and she is afraid she will get light-headed and wobbly on those stairs. Leike spends a bit of time upstairs, probably helping her do her bedtime routine and getting into bed without falling and breaking her neck! Leike signals me to come upstairs to Mrs. V.'s room. She is tucked in like a caterpillar in a cocoon. We both give her kisses and tell her that we love her.

Downstairs Leike whispers, "Helga, I think she hangs around to hear what I am saying when I have people over. We must be careful. I love her dearly, but some days I don't understand her."

We begin to reminisce about our childhood years and how we would ride our bicycles to Nieuwe Meer and swim for hours. Sometimes we would take our clothes off and swim in the nude. I remember how nice it felt having the waves crest against my body. Leike and I became strong swimmers racing each other across the lake. We never made it to the other side, but we had fun trying. I must confess Leike is by far the stronger swimmer. We laugh like school age girls as we talk about the past. Before long, we realize that it is close to curfew time. Leike asks me to stay with her, but I tell her that I can't. I walk up the stairs and gently open Mrs. V.'s bedroom door and hear her snoring like a purring kitten.

"Good night Mrs. V. Thank you for keeping my friend Leike safe and inviting me into your home. May God bless you and protect you," I whisper softly.

After many hugs and kisses, I pedal hard to get home before curfew. I race home in record time. I don't mind having to pedal hard as I was happy to be able to spend extra time with my dear friend Leike.

CHAPTER FOURTEEN

A week after I have supper with Leike I look out from under the blackout curtain hanging in my window and a bright sunny day greets me. The sky is a medium blue shade with white fluffy clouds drifting by on their own schedule. I look at them with envy. I wish I could drift away from this hell. I lift up the blackout curtain and look for my starlings. I have been so occupied with the occupation and the registry that I forget about my feathered little friends. They aren't outside my window but I will look in the Dutch elm tree later. It has a thick patch of leaves that weren't blown off by the bombing. Maybe Mr. and Mrs. Starling have made their home there. I can feel that today is going to be a great day. As Father has said in the past, "It is my responsibility to turn a negative situation into something positive."

After my usual morning routine, I am ready to bicycle to work. I leave fifteen minutes early as I want to check our Dutch elm tree for the birds as well as check on my little flower in the flowerbed. I retrieve my bike and walk it over towards the elm tree. I look up and realize that it has come to life with magnificent foliage decorating the strong branches. I squint and look further into the mass of branches and leaves. Finally, up into the higher branches I see the outline of a nest. I hope that this little home belongs to my little friends.

On my way to work, I stop at the flower bed I visited several days before. I feel compelled to check on my lone little resistant flower. Has it risen above the oppression of weeds and grasses? To my amazement the little plant is doing great. It has grown several more leaves and is looking stronger and healthier. I get off my bike and loosen the soil around the little plant. *"Stay strong my friend,"* I say to myself.

As I turn to leave, I am greeted by a young German soldier. He eyes me suspiciously and asks to see my papers. While looking over my papers, he glances over at the flower bed.

"What were you doing?" He asks me, pointing to the flower bed.

"I was helping a little flower survive in the flower bed. It is being choked out by weeds and grasses around it. I can show you what I have done."

His stern glare softens, and he laughs. "It is ok Fraulein Helga. Where are you going?"

"I am going to my job at the Central Registry."

"You do know that a pretty Dutch girl like you should have a German man like me to protect you."

I thank him for his kind words and slowly walk up to him and give him a kiss on his cheek. I whisper "Auf Wiedersehen" in his ear and walk towards my bike. I look over my shoulder and see the remnants of my red lipstick kiss on his cheek.

Since I completed the Gestapo test, I have been given more independence and my work is not as scrutinized as it was before. The Nazis announce on the radio and in newspapers that all individuals that are fifteen years of age and older are required to now carry an identification card. How many fifteen-year-olds have proper identification? I organize myself at the front desk in anticipation of a busy day. Before our day begins. I look out our window and see a line of people snaking around our building. I stand at the window for a few minutes and see German soldiers and the NSB amusing themselves by controlling the line of people in their own cruel way. I am mortified that they are beating anyone who steps out of position in the line. I hear screams from outside. I have had enough of this shit! I stomp to Boumer's office and barge into his office. Thankfully he is by himself.

"Herr Boumer, German soldiers and the NSB thugs are beating people who are in line to get into this building. Make them stop!"

"My dear Helga, they are probably just Jews."

"Just Jews? What if there are innocent Dutch people getting hurt? Can you go downstairs and get them to stop?"

"Well, darling, I will do this for you and only you because I care about you. Now come over here beside me."

I know what is in store, but I will sacrifice my body in order to stop those fuckers outside. I walk over to him and he redirects my body beside his desk, out of view from prying eyes. He takes his left hand and runs it up my leg, over my stockings to my panties. I take a deep breath as he runs his fingertips over the edge of my panties.

"My Helga, I want to taste you." He says as he puts his finger inside me and his right-hand slips under my panties grabbing my ass. He moans and then puts his finger in his mouth. "My gosh, Helga you taste amazing."

Disgusted with what he just did to me I pipe up. "Herr Boumer, you got what you wanted from me. Now please, stop the senseless beatings outside."

He looks at me and smiles. "I want you darling," he says as he walks towards the door of his office and heads outside.

I walk away not saying a word. I watch out the window as he speaks to the goons. An elderly lady arrives at the counter crying hysterically. She explains that she and her husband were waiting in the line and one of the soldiers took her husband away. They have been married for fifty years and have never been apart.

"*Fuck, I hate these Nazis.*" I say to myself. I am not going to give Boumer anymore of my body today. I signal to a family standing behind her and ask if they can help her out. As I have done in the past, I instruct the family and this kind old woman to go to the police station to find out what has happened to her husband. I know that speaking in Yiddish can make them feel better, but I feel guilty for giving them a false sense of hope. The Nazis will be heartless but, if they are lucky, they may be able to bribe the odd officer. May God protect them - Got zol zey bentshn.

The flow of people is nonstop throughout the day and the many bloodied and bruised faces are a blur. I look to the side and see my colleague, Leos, give several people blank census and identification cards. No words are exchanged between them. The individuals leave the counter with their heads down and scurry down the stairs and out of sight. I pull Leos aside and whisper in her ear that she has to be more subtle in her exchanges. I tell her I will not say a word nor will I question her actions. I add that if I am questioned about any of her actions, I will deny knowing anything. I understand what she is doing.

She smiles and nods. I am not sure if Leos is a spy or a Nazi collaborator. What she did in front of me in my eyes was a stupid risky stunt. Her actions give me more reasons to be extra careful. I will have to ask her if she is aware of my test by the Nazis and Boumer. I still have to test her to see if she is who she claims to be or is she a collaborator with a Dutch accent. I will have her back 100% once she proves to me that she is trustworthy.

CHAPTER FIFTEEN

Today is a very emotional day. I feel like a fifthly whore for allowing Boumer to touch and penetrate my body. Yet, I did stop the malicious acts of the Nazi and NSB thugs. Have I set a precedence with him? I hope not. Yet, my inner voice keeps reminding me that I have to get access to the hidden room. I am successful in ignoring Boumer all day. I spend all of my time at the counter with Leos doing our jobs. Leos has not mentioned anything about spy work, and I don't ask any questions. Knowledge can be a death sentence in Nazi occupied Amsterdam. I leave work abruptly to avoid seeing Boumer. I realize I left my sweater at my desk but that is fine. I am smart enough to bring my purse to the front counter so I can escape his sexual advances.

Father is home for dinner again. I am starting to worry about him. Why the change in behavior? I know something is bothering him as he is pacing up and down our hallway floor. *"My gosh Father,"* I say to myself, *"You are going to erode our wooden floors."* I know that Father will talk when he wants to. Olga is very creative in her meal preparation once again. Tonight, we have potatoes, beets, and onions in a cheese sauce and homemade white bread. We all eat ample portions so there isn't any room for dessert.

Father retires to the teak sofa and asks everyone to join him. Now he is ready to talk.

"Today, I went to the bank and withdrew most of our money and emptied our safety deposit boxes. I anticipate that it will be just a matter of time before the Nazis start pilfering our assets. I have our birth certificates, marriage certificate, Olga's and Lukasz's paperwork, and jewelry willed to your mother. Also, we have several stunning pieces of jewelry which several of Mother's wealthy clients gave her for making them the beautiful gowns which she has. Now, we need to find a place to hide these items. Lukasz, how are the hidden rooms progressing?"

Before Lukasz can say anything, I excuse myself.

"Father, Mother, Olga, and Lukasz, I don't want to know anything about these hidden rooms. I am working in the lion's den with Nazis sniffing around every corner looking for spies or anyone that they deem is suspicious. I will ask you to let me know when the time is right. Good night."

The adults continue to talk in lower voices as I go up to my bedroom.

CHAPTER SIXTEEN

F ather invites some of his co-workers, Dr Dahe and Dr. Dyker along with his wife Kate, over for dinner. Dr. Dahe is a young doctor who was fortunate enough to graduate medical school before the occupation. He is a looker; tall with dark hair, piercing blue eyes, porcelain skin, and an amazing smile. He has sexy dimples in the left side of his cheek. He is dressed in a tailored gray suit with a cream-colored shirt and navy-blue geometric tie. Dr. Dyker is wearing a tailored brown suit with a white dress shirt and a green and light brown checkered tie while Mrs. Dyker is wearing one of mother's creations. An elegant peach colored gown with long layers of chiffon hanging down past an empire waist. The sweetheart neckline is adorned with cinched bows with rhinestones. Mother is wearing one of her dark purple chiffon creations and I am wearing a black off the shoulder gown with white collar and bustle bow which she also made. Olga assisted me in styling my hair into soft waves that accent my face like a picture frame enhances an exquisite piece of art.

Dr. Dahe and I let the 'adults' talk as we sit on the teak couch in the parlor. I find it very awkward; we are both guarded with our conversation and body language. I guess it is a sign of the times as one never knows if the person you are communicating with is a spy. Olga senses a bit of tension in the air and offers us each a glass of Chardonnay.

The wine is the perfect relaxer and within a few minutes we are talking, though still cautious of the words we speak.

Dr. Dahe's parents are Russian and they moved to Amsterdam when he was a child. When he first attended early grade school, he could not speak Dutch. But with the aid of a tutor, he quickly became fluent in Dutch and his family made sure that he kept up his Russian. I speak to him in Russian and ask how he enjoys being a doctor. He isn't surprised that I speak his language. I assume Father told him about my ability to speak and write Russian. Olga refills our half drank glasses of Chardonnay.

I tell him about my family and my language skills. I touch a bit on working at the registry. He comments that he has to update his census and identification card. I wish I knew him more as I would caution him on his Russian background and that it will raise red flags with the Nazis. Maybe after dinner I will tell him.

Olga is preparing a German dinner to the best of her ability. Despite the rations between our black-market connections, and the harvesting and preserving of the vegetables we did in the early fall we have enough food for a wonderful meal. She creates an amazing Eintopfsonntage which is a one pot meal. Lukasz was able to get his hands on a little chicken to add to the meal which consists of potatoes, onions, carrots, and canned tomatoes. Olga is an expert at spicing any meal she makes. I wish I knew what her concoctions are, but I am not sure she even knows. She serves the dish with freshly made Kommißbrot, which is a dark German bread. She has set the table with fine Austrian crystal glasses, polished silverware, and fine English china. It is a setting for royalty. Olga and Lukasz are never excluded from any of our meals as they are part of our family. The dinner conversations are light and uplifting for the situation. I truly believe that nobody wants to ruin a beautiful dinner with the talk of the Nazis. Compliments are flowing for Olga and her beautifully prepared meal. I assist Olga in clearing the dinner plates and then we bring out her famous apple dessert complete with a dollop cream. Father has selected a bottle of Clio champagne to pair with dessert. It is perfectly chilled to accent our exquisite dessert. I look over at Dr. Dahe and see that he is savoring every morsel and I can imagine the champagne bubbles dancing in his mouth.

After dessert, Olga and I clear the table. Mother socializes with Kate and they slip into her dressmaking room, each with a champagne flute full of the bubbly magic. Dr Dahe, who instructs me to call him Karl, surprises Olga and I when he offers to assist in the clean up. Wow, very impressive Karl. Meanwhile Father retrieves a bottle of Cognac from the cellar for after-dinner drinks. He grabs his special glasses from our china cabinet and pours himself, Dr. Dyker, and Karl a drink from his prized bottle. He announces to the adults within ear reach that this is his last bottle and he can't see himself travelling to France anytime soon to restore his cellar. The adults laugh but we all know that what he is saying is correct as shortly after occupation, the Nazis closed our borders.

While the adults engage in their gossip, talks of politics, and whatever else came to mind, Karl and I sit at the dinner room table beside each other. We talk and laugh like teenagers. He admits to me that he is a communist and he has no use for the Nazis. I warm him to be careful about using the "C" word as there are spies everywhere. I look over at the dining room window and am thankful that it is not open.

His comment is simple and to the point, "I am aware."

"Karl, why did you reveal your darkest secret to me?"

"Helga, first of all it's not my darkest secret. There is something about you that makes me trust you. I can't put my finger on it."

"Could it be that I work at the registry and am privy to lots of Nazi secrets?"

"No, Helga, it is what I see in your eyes and your soul."

With that he leans over and delicately kisses me on my left cheek. He smells very good. I am afraid to turn my face toward him. The kiss breaks the ice and I tell him about the registry and the Nazi's views on Russians.

"Karl, I must warn you. The Nazis are doing something secretly with our census cards. I have not been able to learn what it is yet and advise you not to update your cards until I know what is going on. It is the fear of the unknown that frightens me."

"Thank you for the good advice Helga. I will hold off until I hear from you. Does that mean that I can see you again?"

I smile and nod my head.

Shortly after the stolen kiss, Father announces that our guests should leave now before the curfew. As we are constantly reminded there are serious repercussions for anyone caught out past curfew. Kate leaves mother's dressmaking room with a huge smile on her face. While the two women were in mother's dressmaking room, mother made her a beautiful peach scarf with flecks of gold spattered throughout it. Father, Olga, and I help our guests with their coats, hats, and boots. Karl kisses me on my hand and whispers in my ear that he hopes to see me soon.

I think to myself, *"Karl I do also."*

CHAPTER SEVENTEEN

True to his word, Karl telephones me several days later. I agree to meet him at Café Mand Zeed which is located in the red-light district. This café is, up to now, a safe place for homosexuals, lesbians, and straight patrons to intermix. I know the owner very well and she has informed me that regular German Wehrmacht soldiers are not allowed in the café or in the red-light district. Yet, it is not uncommon to see senior German Officers enjoying several drinks while mingling with any woman that will give them the time of day.

As we enter the café, it is filled with cigarette smoke and the sound of loud voices and cheers. One of the regular senior German Officers is celebrating his birthday. The atmosphere is one that reminisces of before war. The drinks are flowing, music is playing, and people are dancing. The older German Officer is surrounded by beautiful woman who are feeding him drinks and flirting with him. I know several of those women and they are lesbians. I know that with the occupation, lesbians have to blend into Nazi society. Somehow Miss Van Smythe has been able to get her hands on some chocolate, exotic fruits, cheese, and crackers for the occasion. I think that this German Officer has taken a shine to Miss Van Smythe and assisted with the party food. He probably does not realize she favors the sensual touch of a woman over that of a man.

I look at Miss Van Smythe and she points to a secluded table in the corner. As we walk by the German Officer's table, he grabs me by my waist and sets me on his lap. Karl looks in disgust and I signal to him that I can handle this. I place my arm around this Nazi and I give him a kiss on his lips. I say "Alles Gute zum Geburtstag, Sir" (Happy Birthday Sir) to him and then he magically lets me go. I quickly jump off his lap and head to Karl who is impatiently waiting for me at our designated table.

"Karl, I apologize for my behavior but that Nazi pig is a regular at the cafe. I don't trust him at all. So, it is best to apease him with a little kiss. Now, I need to rinse the Nazi filth from my mouth." Miss Van Smythe brings Karl and I a stein of beer and a glass of water. I turn my body to the side, away from prying eyes, I gargle water in my mouth and spit it into my napkin. There, that should remove any Nazism from my mouth!

Karl laughs and gives me a hug and a kiss. He looks toward the other side of the cafe in hopes that the arrogant birthday swine is watching him mark his territory like a pedigree dog claiming his mate.

Karl and I are opening up more to each other. He is very intelligent and comes from an affluent family. His father is a very reputable criminal lawyer, and, in the past, he has defended NSB members who have been caught acting inappropriately above the law. Karl mentions that his father verbally expresses his support for the Nazis and their eugenics program. He also makes it known loud and clear, to whoever is in ears range, that he hates the Jews, the cancers of society. I look at Karl in disbelief.

I whisper to him. "How can your father be pro-Nazi when he is a communist. Is he a Nazi collaborator? Doesn't he know that the Nazis hate communists and Jews and wants to eliminate these people, including you and your family?"

"Yes, Helga, he is aware, but I think he does it for show and not to draw attention to him or our family. My mother stays at home and spends her time socializing with influential ladies. I believe that your mother has made mom one of her evening gowns."

Now I am very confused and I know I need truthful answers and Karl may not speak them now. Instead, I decide to play it safe.

"Karl, you and your father are playing a dangerous game with the Nazis. Be careful."

I didn't give him a chance to respond as I gulp down my beer and announce that it is time to get home. Could he please give me a ride home? As we leave Miss Van Smythe gives me a smile and I give her the hand gesture that I am unsure if this man is safe.

On the drive home, I thank Karl for a wonderful night. At my house, I allow him to walk me to the front door. I quickly open the front door and he gives me a quick kiss and says he will call me later.

I reply with sure.

I go inside and realize that I am very suspicious and paranoid of anyone these days. The only thing I can do is check his census card to see if he is telling the truth or not. Father may like him, but he is not a bloodhound and he cannot sniff out a collaborator if his life depends upon it.

I say goodnight to Mother and Father who are sitting by the wood burning stove. I wash my face, change into my night dress, and hit my pillow. Before I know it, it is morning.

CHAPTER EIGHTEEN

I wake up and instantly start to think of Karl. He is a nice man but is this just a facade to draw me into his web of lies? Or is he a genuine handsome communist man who is sincere in his words and actions? After the usual morning routine, I jump on my bike with one mission in mind…to read Karl's census card. On my route, I see many German soldiers and the dreaded NSB thugs. Out of nowhere, one of the dreaded NBS thugs jumps out in front of me. I lose my balance and fall on the road scraping my left knee. A little stream of blood is flowing down my leg.

I am furious! I look at the idiot that jumped in front of me and yell, "Who the fuck do you think you are?"

I look past the NSB uniform and into the eyes of the asshole. I recognize these piercing eyes. These are the eyes of Bram Van der Venden. Bram is an annoying bully who, unfortunately, was in all of my classes growing up. What he lacked in brains, which was lots, he made up with his attitude and fists. He always had a crowd of wannabes around him and he always picked on me. I have long hair and in school he would pull my braids and push me down. Many times, I would come home from school in tears with bruises and cuts.

Lukasz taught me how to defend myself and throw strategically placed punches or kicks. He was my personal self-defense coach. Mother is against a lady fighting and insisted that I stop acting like a boy. Lukasz and I worked around her schedule and I became stronger and smarter with my kicks and punches. All the sneaking around worked. I finally beat him at his game as one time, I kicked and punched him and gave the creep a black eye. He never bothered me after that. I thought I had beaten my menace for good but then puberty hit. He was still a bully but a horny bully walking around stroking the outside of his trousers at his groin area. He was sickening and disgusting. Yuck, the thought of having that walking erection touch my body sent shivers through my body.

"Ms. Helga, you must be more careful," he said slyly with a twinkle in his eyes.

"You are the one who jumped in front of me."

"Oh, by the way I need to see your identification card. Hey boys, maybe I will search her body as she does look suspicious!"

His new group of bullies' snicker at that notion.

"Bram, you are still a fucking bully."

"Yes, Helga, but I am now a bully with power!"

"Asshole!" I exclaim as I hand him my identification card which he takes his time inspecting.

"It looks genuine," he snickers.

I know that I can't do a thing about any of his actions. He is now a member of the dreaded NSB. He walks closer to me and runs his hands over my blouse touching my breasts.

"Oh my, Ms. Helga, you have developed into quite the beautiful woman."

"You sick bastard, leave me alone!" I shout sternly at him and look him in the eye.

"Oh, by the way, do you have a permit for your bicycle?"

"Braum, I don't have a permit. I work at the registry."

"Helga, I know where you work and I know all about you. WHERE IS YOUR BICYCLE PERMIT?" He yells. "You are not an essential worker so, you lose it. I will be nice and let you retrieve your personal belongings from the basket."

I push him aside and retrieve my purse.

"You know Helga, I can arrest you for pushing me, but I won't. I enjoy it too much." He whispers in my ears as he grabs the front of his pants.

"Get out of my way!"

"As you wish Ms. Helga. The next time I stop you, you will be mine. He smiles sheepishly and smacks his hands together. "Have a nice walk!" He yells to me as I walk away. I can hear his cronies laughing.

Humiliated, I walk away.

I no longer care if I am late for work. I will tell Boumer what the NSB did to me. Maybe he can get my bicycle back. I wipe the blood trinkling down my leg. I apply pressure to the scratch hoping to stop the bleeding. Oh well, it's only a scrape. I arrive at work fifty minutes late. Leos looks at me as I ascend the stairs excusing myself for trying to get by the line of people. I nod that I am alright and I go straight to Boumer's office to explain why I am late.

"Helga, are you alright?" He looks up at me from his paperwork and then sees my bloody leg.

"What happened?"

I give him a detailed description of my experience with Braum and how he confiscated my bike. He walks over to me and gives me a hug. "Let's get your wound cleaned up."

He walks out of his office and instructs his secretary to get a damp cloth with soap on it. "The NSB roughed up Helga and took her bicycle".

Next thing I know there is a procession of my colleagues checking on me and giving me hugs. I wasn't expecting this type of comradery from my colleagues. Maybe this is the hammer to break the iciness in the office. While one of my colleagues is playing nurse, Boumer calls his contact in the SS to get my bike back.

"Oh, I pray that they reprimand Braum." I say to myself.

My bandage on my war wound is secure. Back to work I go.

The first thing I do is check Karl and his father's census cards. Everything looks in order. I must give Karl's parents credit as they did not record his Russian heritage on his card. But a smart investigator can put two and two together.

I hope I get my bicycle returned as I know Boumer will offer to give me a ride home if I don't. I don't welcome that as I know that he will have his Nazi paws all over me. Near the end of the day, he comes out to the front desk and tells me to follow him to his office.

"Fraulein Helga, your bicycle is waiting for you outside. The NSB person, Braum Van der Venden has been reprimanded and you don't have to worry about him bothering you again."

I thank Boumer and he walks towards me, clearly wanting more than a thank you. I give him a quick hug and kiss on the cheek and dart out of his office. I look back and he has a sinister smile on his face. I know that I owe him more than what I just gave him. Fuck! I thank all of my colleagues again for their support and leap down the stairs to my bicycle. Ha-ha Braum. Fuck you! I got even, again!

Once, I arrive at my home, I do not want to ring alarm bells by showing mother my little wound. I tell Olga what happened and she smiles at me and gives me a hug.

"Yes, Helga, you are a smart and strong woman. Still, you must be careful on who you trust. It is unfortunate that you have to use your body to keep on your boss's good side. Be smart. Helga, I like Mr. Karl. I did speak to him in Russian the last time he was here. He seems like a nice man. Be careful just the same."

"I love you Olga. Do you have any wine handy?"

She laughs and goes into the kitchen, the next thing I hear is the wonderful pop of a champagne cork releasing its bubbling contents. Aww, music to my ears. Father is working late at the hospital and Mother eats her meal in her dressmaking room. It's just Olga, Lukasz, and I. I tell Lukasz what happened and the look on his face indicates that he's worried. He doesn't say a word.

After I clean up and an after-dinner glass of champagne, I curl up on my bed and read a book banned by the Nazis, *The Green Hills of Africa* by Ernest Hemingway.

CHAPTER NINETEEN

I wake up curled in a ball with my book beside me. Today, I am going to test Karl's loyalty to The Netherlands, and subsequently me, or the Nazis. It is a Saturday, June 29th and I feel compelled to engage in an act of resistance. Today is Prince Bernhard's birthday and he is known to wear a white carnation in his suit lapel. I know there will be crowds of people at our Queen's statue.

I call Karl and ask him to pick me up at 09:00. I tell him I want to go to Yvo's floating flower stall in the Singel Canal. Yvo is a long-time friend of my family and she always prepares wonderful floral arrangements for Mother and Father's lavish parties. Karl parks his car and we walk to Yvo's stall. She sees Karl and I walking toward her stall and has an ear to ear grin and yells to me, "Helga darling, you look amazing!"

"So, do you, Yvo, I yell back."

I introduce her to Karl and she shows us the flowers and gifts she is selling. I tell her that I want to buy ten white carnations with angelic wings and two large fragrant red roses. She looks at Karl and then me. I give her the 'I'm not sure if I can trust him' signal. I whisper to her that I want Karl and I to strategically place white carnations at businesses. It is my subtle form of resistance.

Yvo places her finger to her lip to be quiet. A few minute later, she brings me my beautiful flowers. Karl pays for them and we both give

Yvo goodbye hugs. As we walk away from the canal, I ask Karl if he knows what the flowers are for? I think he suspects that I am up to something.

"Helga, darling, from the sparkle in your eyes, I know that these flowers are not for your kitchen table."

"Karl, you are correct. As you may or may not be aware it is Prince Bernd's birthday and to show support to the Dutch Royal Family, we are going to place a white carnation at businesses, and I have one special business in mind to place the red roses."

"Ok, Helga, let's do it!"

I feel guilty for not asking Leike to join us. I need to find out if I can trust Karl or not. Plus, Leike will be too possessive of me and will give away our dangerous secret.

As we walk along Hontubger Street, Karl and I strategically place carnations outside of businesses on their doorstep unless the business owner waves me in. I must say that Karl impresses me, he is a willing participant. We laugh and joke about silly things. We walk up to Van Der Holtr ice cream and chocolate shop. Mr. and Mrs. Van Der Holtr make the best ice cream in the Netherlands. We drop in, exchange greetings and introductions and ask them both if they would like two white patriotic carnations and two red roses. Like lightning Mrs. Van Der Holtr retrieves a vase from the back area. As she is arranging her little bouquet, Mr. Van Der Holtr offers us each an ice cream cone.

"Miss Helga and Mr. Karl do not look at the list of ice cream flavours we have listed. These are for the German soldiers and their Dutch whores. The ice cream is of inferior quality. These occupiers and collaborators love it. I hide the good ice cream in the back. How does a rich Belgium chocolate ice cream cone sound to you both? And don't even think of paying me for them, the flowers speak volumes on both of your integrities."

We keep our conversation short just in case of spies lurking around. We exchange warm goodbyes before we leave. Karl and I have three more carnations to deliver. As we are walking, he tries to hold my hand. I pull my hand away and stop Karl in his tracks.

"Karl, I must tell you something about me. It is very important for you to know this as I don't want to mislead you."

"Helga, darling, you are an amazing strong beautiful woman. Your level of intellect entices me. I am growing fond of you and I want to protect you."

"Oh Karl, thank you for your kind words. Let's take our relationship one step at a time."

He puts his arms around me and hugs me tightly. "Helga, my dear, nobody will ever hurt you. Darling, lets distribute the rest of these flowers and then I will take you home."

"Karl, I don't want this day to end."

"Helga, I didn't say that I was dropping you off and going home. I will stay with you for as long as you like."

"That sounds great."

We walk to his car with his arm around me. Inside I am confused, my heart is pounding not due to fear but for the lust I have for Karl.

Father isn't home so Olga and Mother greet us at the door. Both have incredibly huge smiles on their faces. Olga has some bread and meat left over from dinner. She explains that they ate early as Mother has to finish Mrs. Vossom's dress for tomorrow. Ah, the famous mayor wife's dress.

Olga opens a bottle of Chardonnay which Karl and I sip with our meal. We talk about our day of being defiant persons distributing Dutch propaganda. Olga interrupts us and says that she heard that twenty people were arrested at the Queen's statue for carrying carnations and yelling anti-Nazi slogans.

"Olga, I will check at work to see if anyone knows anything."

"Helga, how can people be so careless and shout those slogans. Don't they realize that they could be arrested?"

"I know Olga, but I think people are sick of the occupation with it's curfew, rations, and disintegrations of our freedoms."

"Karl, I have to ask you something important."

"Go ahead darling".

I like the sound of that from his mouth. "I have noticed that many of the death certificates of Jewish men and women state the cause of death as heart issues. I find it odd that a young Jewish woman died from a heart issue."

Karl looks at me sternly. "Helga, what I am going to tell you, you cannot repeat to anyone. The Nazis are beginning to implement their twisted medical polices at the hospital. They only want us to tend to Aryan patients. The thing is, I treat all my patients equally, but I can't be beside them all the time. I had left a non-Aryan patient who is recovering from an injury and when I got into the hospital in the morning, I was informed that she passed away during the night due to an undiagnosed heart issue. I knew something wasn't right, so I visited our hospital doctor who works in the morgue. I questioned him about it and he said for me to drop it or I could be next. Helga," he says with tears forming in his eyes, "the Nazis are killing newborn babies and there is nothing I can do about it."

Even though it is very unladylike I sit on Karl's lap and hold him. "Karl, my love, you are a good man. You can help patients when you can. But remember, you have to protect yourself for your father and for me."

I wipe the tears cascading down his face and give him a big kiss. He responds with an intense yet intimate kiss. Wow, the man is a great kisser.

"Helga, I fell in love with you the first time I saw you."

"Karl, I have the same feelings."

Mother comes out of dressmaking room and informs me it is time for me to model Mrs. Vossom's dress.

"Karl, do you mind?"

"I look forward to seeing my lady in a fancy dress."

I skip to the dressmaking room where I strip to my brassier and panties. I slip on Mrs. Vossom's gown and it fits perfectly. I look in the mirror and see I have transformed into a goddess. Mother does her fidgeting with the dress, checking to make sure everything is completed to perfection. She is a perfectionist with her creations. I just want to go out and show Karl how I look. Finally, after what seems like forever, to an impatient woman, mother allows me to show Karl my new look. I walk out of the room and spin around in front of Karl. I look down and see my dress flow like a magic carpet gliding in the wind.

Karl puts his arms around me and whispers, "My gosh you are beautiful." He kisses me on my cheek.

Mother pipes up, "No kissing in my dress, I don't need drool stains on my dress. Helga, come here and get changed please."

"Mrs. Berta, the dress is beautiful."

"Thank you, Karl."

After changing, Karl and I go into the parlor. We laugh and sip wine while we cuddle on the couch. I look over at the clock and realize it is getting late.

"Karl, it is getting close to the curfew."

"Helga, I am fine. I have a special pass because I am a doctor. I can always say I was visiting an ill patient.

"Am I ill Karl?"

"Yes, my love, I want to fix your heart."

"Well, I think I need to have many home visits to make sure that my heart is getting better."

"Yes, my love, as many as you want."

Time goes by quickly when you are cuddling with your man. Before we know it, it is past midnight.

"Darling, you should get to bed. I have to work tomorrow, and I will call you when I can. Goodbye my princess."

After he leaves, I clean up our wine glasses. The house is quiet except for Mother humming in her sanctuary. I float up the stairs to my bedroom with a smile on my face. Sweet dreams my love Karl. Goodnight.

CHAPTER TWENTY

This morning I witness the true nature of the Nazis. The Waal wall is located behind our building and our back-office windows face it. I can hear shouts, shots, and barking dogs. Leos covers for me as I want to see what these horrific noises are about. I look out the window and see German Wehrmacht soldiers and NSB thugs herding Dutchmen into the square. They are beating these men with the handles of their bayonets and their fists. Several of the soldiers are vicious as they poke the Dutchmen with the bayonet ensuring that they draw blood. If anyone falls, they are greeted with a volley of merciless kicks. What the hell is going on?

I go into Boumer's office and ask him what the hell is going on? He looks up at me and informs me matter of fact that these men were arrested in retaliation of the resistance.

"What did the resistance do?" My question is ignored. Again, I ask, "What did the resistance do? Where are these men going?"

I can tell by the look on his face and his body language that Boumer is getting quite annoyed at me.

"Listen Helga, I am not at liberty to answer your questions. Return to your desk immediately. The SS will bring you the paperwork to update these men's cards."

I look at him in disbelief and disgust.

"Don't just stand there Helga, move your nice ass and go do your job!! Close the door behind you when you leave as I don't want to be disturbed."

Under my breath, I am saying Fuck You. I slam his door shut and walk away. He is as unpredictable as a hydrogen atom. I know that I have to quit getting emotional when people are rounded up the by Nazis; but it is in my nature. But what I will do is quit telling Mother and Father about my day at the registry. I don't need Mother spinning out of control and Father having to deal with her. I will keep Olga and Lukasz up to date as they are the rational people in our household.

The day drags on as I carefully venture to the back window to see what is happening now and then. At one point they have the men standing in a line and are loading them onto trucks. Where the hell are they taking these men? How do they know who to select for retaliation against the resistance?

An SS officer arrives with a list of the Dutchmen they grabbed. I look at the man in disgust. "You Nazi thug, how dare you grab innocent Dutchmen!"

He looks at me sternly. "Fraulein it is best you shut your mouth or you will be next!"

Leos grabs my arm and says, "Let it go, it isn't worth it".

The officer continues to stand in front of us, looking at us both. He does the Hitler salute and says, "Heil Hitler".

Leos nudges me in the ribs and we both respond. We look at the line of people who are frightened by what they just witnessed. We both refocus and help the people in line. At the end of work, I thank Leos for stopping me from getting into serious trouble from the SS office. We hug, smile, and leave work.

Tonight Mr. and Mrs. Vossom come over to the house after dinner. Mrs. Vossom is trying on the masterpiece that mother created for her. Father is strategically home from his hospital shift early. While Mrs. Vossom is getting the final touches, if any are needed, on her dress, Father, Mr. Vossom, and I relax in the parlor.

"Lars, I apologize for the way I acted when Helga was ordered to report to the registry. I did not have a choice as I was and still am at mercy of the Gestapo."

"I understand that your hands are tied," I respond sympathetically to him.

"Lars and Helga, the Nazis will be implementing severe decrees on us. There is talk of a decrease with our rations as they want more food, fuel, medicine, whatever they can get their hands on sent to Germany. They also want to move and restrict the Jews to the Jewish Quarter and exterminate them. Also, there is talk of sending Dutch men and women to work in German factories."

"Where did you hear this? When will it happen?" I quiz the mayor.

"I have overhead these discussions in my office. I am invited into the conference room and asked my opinion. Of course, I have to tell them what they want to hear. I know they are in the planning process and these actions could occur as early as January next year."

I tell Father and Mr. Vossom what I saw today, both are surprised.

"I know that the Nazis are worried about the resistance and their goal is turn the Dutch people against it. Helga, this is what you witnessed today. We must be alert and aware of our surroundings. If I learn anything, I will somehow keep you and Helga updated on what the Nazis are up to."

"That is nice, but if you are under surveillance with the Nazis, it is best you keep your distance from us. I need to keep my family safe"

"I understand Lars. I will be careful but will what I can do. Please keep what I told you both today secret."

Mrs. Vossom flows out of mother's room with her elegant gown. She looks beautiful. Her husband's mouth drops and he walks over and hugs his wife. Mother quickly separates the two lovebirds and says she wants to package the dress.

The dress is neatly wrapped, money is exchanged, and the Vossoms say goodbye.

"Berta, you did a magnificent job on her dress. I am so proud of you."

"Thank you, Lars, I am exhausted and off to bed."

After Mother goes to bed, Father and I whisper about what we heard. Neither of us are surprised about what could be in store for us in 1941 and onward.

"Father, I believe that the key to these roundups are in the secret room at the registry. How can the Nazis know which men to grab and if they will be home?"

"I think you are right Helga, but again, we must be cautious in our words and actions."

"I agree Father. It has been a long day and I am very tired."

"Goodnight Helga."

CHAPTER TWENTY-ONE

I t is finally December 24 and we are preparing for our Christmas celebration. The Nazis have outlawed Christmas and other religious celebrations. We laugh at these restrictions as we will never forfeit Christmas for the Nazis!

Karl and I are an item. We see each other on a regular basis. Karl offers to help Lukasz find the perfect Christmas tree. The guys are out for half the day and come back with a small kerstbomen (Christmas tree). Our little scots pine is approximately 1.5 meters high. Olga grabs a bucket from the garden shed, pours water in it and places our little kerstbomen in it. The little tree looks smaller in the bucket.

Even though we have our blackout curtains in place we are aware there are Nazis and spies everywhere. We descend down the stairs to our cellar and secure our little tree to a vertical beam.

Father jokingly says, "Let's decorate the Christmas tree with swastikas and put Hitler's picture on the top."

"Father that sounds great," I comment excitedly. "Maybe we can burn the edges around the picture and shove the top tree branch up his ass!"

Everyone laughs hysterically. Everyone participates in decorating our little tree with Mother's collection of decorations or from each of our own personal collections. To my surprise, Karl has one ornament he places on the tree. It is a small beautiful navy-blue box beautifully decorated with gold sequins and a gorgeous lace gold ribbon. I recognize the workmanship as something that Yvo would make. I had invited Leike to our celebration, but she is spending a quiet Christmas with Mrs. V. We also invited Karl's parents, but they kindly declined. When I ask Karl about it, he shrugs his shoulders and comments "That is Dad!"

Our whole family, including Karl work hard to get our Christmas dinner ingredients. Mother and Olga work on their Christmas dinner wish list which includes eggs, flour, sugar, almonds, cheeses, sliced meats, nuts, dried fruits, venison, and yeast. The rest of the ingredients are in our basement. Between the ration cards, friends, and black market we did it.

Tomorrow is December 25th, which is the first day of Christmas celebrations. After the tree is decorated and a couple glasses of Chardonnay, it is bedtime. Karl is staying the night, but he is strategically sleeping in a room between me and my parents.

In the morning, Olga makes a delicious breakfast with almond paste bread, different cheeses, sliced meats, and champagne. The food is on separate plates so everyone helps him or herself. Karl is mesmerized by the food. He whispers to me that mother and Olga are amazing cooks. I taunt Karl and tell him that they taught me how to cook.

"Mmmm," he responds with a wink.

Mother is busy making Kerstransjes wreath cookies to place on our little 'resistance' tree and to eat. I am kicked out of the kitchen for trying to steal yummy raw cookie batter. Our Christmas dinner is venison, potatoes, carrots, beets, turnip, goose, hare, Kerstbrood (Christmas bread) and banketstaaf for dessert. Father selects a Bordeaux blend red for dinner and a Dutch advocaat to pair with our dessert.

AFTER DINNER we sing forbidden Dutch Christmas songs. We know that if we are heard we could be reported to the Gestapo and taken away, but we don't care. With the fireplace roaring in the parlor, we sit drinking a bottle of Father's Clio champagne and sing Sinterklaas and Goed Heilig Mank (Saint Nicholas, Good Holy Man). We all realize that this could be the last time we spend Christmas together. Karl excuses himself and heads for the basement. He retrieves the beautiful navy-blue box and hands it to me.

"Helga, my love this is for you. I love you with all my heart."

I unwrap the box and inside is a beautiful ring. There is a large diamond in the middle which is surrounded by rubies.

"Helga, this is my grandmother's ring and I want you to be my wife. Your father has given me permission to ask you to marry me. Will you marry me darling?"

"Yes, I will my love!"

He places the ring on my finger and gives me a big kiss. Mother and Olga are in tears. Karl and I hug Mother and Olga together and Father and Lukasz separately. Now, I look forward to the future.

CHAPTER TWENTY-TWO

As the hands on the clock slowly move towards midnight, I pray that this coming year will be more humane than the past year. I know that Happy New Year has a new meaning in Nazi occupied Amsterdam. I know that I am happy when the front door of our house is not kicked in by the Nazis. I am happy that I or members of my family have not been arrested. I am happy that the bakery is not out of bread when I reach the front of the line.

I know that the Nazis will continue to tighten the noose around the Dutch people and our country. Karl has witnessed the convoy of trucks laden with Dutch food, fuel, and textiles heading to the train station to be transported to Germany. It is a known fact that the Nazis pillage us to feed their war machine and their population. They are eroding the quality of life we once enjoyed as free Dutch men and women.

Today, the future Mrs. Karl rides her bike to work. My cute dresses and skirts have been replaced with a pair of brown utility pants, a starched blouse covered by one of Olga's knitted sweaters, warm wool socks and bulky boots that are two sizes too big for my feet but are needed to accommodate my socks. My exoskeleton consists of a long wool blend chocolate colored coat, matching hat, and mitts and the finishing touch is a warm knitted scarf that I can wrap around my neck two times. I must look overdressed to the privilege ones riding in their toasty warm vehicles, but I don't care. I am dressing for comfort not fashion. Even when I am dressed in these layers, I can feel the crisp northern winter wind striking me ferociously across the face like pins piercing a pin cushion when I ride my bicycle to the registry.

Last night Mother Nature gave us a dusting of snow accompanied by a brisk northern wind. I have completed about .5 km of my ride when I look to the left and see four Wehrmacht soldiers about fifty meters from where I am. Curiosity has got the best of me so I drop my bike and walk to a small stand of pine trees. The wind is still blowing snow in my direction so I place my hand above my eyebrows hoping to shield my eyes from the piercing wind propelling snowflakes into my eyes and face. My eyes adjust to the elements and I see that these four Wehrmacht soldiers are pouring two buckets of water onto a man, woman, and a small child. I see two other soldiers bringing buckets from the canal. I am frozen in place like the water on the snow and I hope that the trees' branches can hide me from these evil soldiers. I watch in horror and disgust as they force the naked man and woman to remain on the ground as they pour more water on them and the little girl who is crawling on her mother.

The mother and father screams are echoing, "Stop, please stop this. What have we done? Please let our little girl live!"

One soldier responds to the plea by dousing the little girl with cold water; she is screaming in Yiddish for her mother and father. They then force the parents to stand as they beat them with the blunt ends of their bayonets and then they take turns piercing their freezing bodies with the sharp ends. The snow is slowly becoming saturated with their blood. The mother tries to grab her child, but one soldier throws her on the snowy ground and repeatedly pokes her with the sharp end of his bayonet. Her shrieks of pain fill the air and hopefully float up to heaven. Blood is seeping in the snow under her little body. The sadistic soldiers laugh and taunt their injured prey. One of the soldiers turns and sees me watching their amusement.

"Hey, Fraulein, look at this."

I watch as he grabs the little girl and swings her by one leg and bashes her head into the tree. He does it several times, until the little girl's head is a mass of blood and tissue. He throws the little girl's silent mangled limp body onto her mother. Her parent's screams ascend to heaven. They are begging for their lives, but their pleas fall on deaf, insensitive ears.

"Fraulein, how do you like your Jew, frozen or tenderized?"

Their laughter is uncontrollable. One soldier shouts out that he has had enough of these wailing filths and shoots the parents in their heads. Two of them drag the bodies in the direction of the canal leaving a blood-soaked trail behind them.

"Fraulein, you have seen enough. Unless you want to end up like the Jews, get the fuck out of here."

I save my ass by giving them the Hitler salute and yell "Heil Hitler!"

I quickly run to my bike and pedal like my life depends upon it. I hate fucking Nazis! I didn't have time to vomit so I swallow my projectile. I fight back my tears, but the dam explodes as tears gush down my face. As I pedal to work, I feel the tears freeze to the exposed areas of my face. I feel my scarf getting moist and freezing in spots from the wind. I don't care! I want to erase the horrors from my mind. But I know this Jewish family and the faces of the Wehrmacht soldiers will be etched in my mind forever.

When I reach the registry building, I am greeted by two of the Wehrmacht soldiers I have become acquainted with. One reaches out to embrace me and I push him away; instead, he opens the door for me speechless. The tears are still flowing down my face and my cries echo in the stairwell hallway. Leos hears me and runs down the stairs to meet me.

"Helga, what is the matter?"

We stop in the middle of stairs and in between tears and sniffles I tell her what I witnessed. "Leos, those bastards must be stopped!"

"I know Helga."

She puts her arm around me and walks me to my desk. The other women look up from their work to see what the commotion is all about. Leos looks at them in disgust and firmly states that I am fine. I walk to my desk to set my belongings down. Boumer comes out of his office, I assume to see what the fuss is all about and asks me if I'm ok.

"I will be once I calm down. I just witnessed another Nazi atrocity!" I reply as the tears continue to flow down my cheeks. I look at him through blood shot teary eyes and tell him what I had witnessed on my way to work.

Boumer looks at me and smugly comments, "Get used to it as it is going to get worse. Now once you have collected your thoughts, I want you to come into my office for a meeting. Leos return to your post out front and assist the filth and Dutch, NOW!"

"You are a heartless bastard." I mumble underneath my breath.

Herr Boumer turns around, gives me an evil look with his glaring eyes staring at me and his thin smile shaped like a razor-sharp knife blade. Then he slams his door shut startling all the women. The women look at me and I don't say a word. It is better to keep quiet in these situations as I still don't know who the collaborators are. I don't even acknowledge their looks. I go into the lavatory to freshen up as best as I can. I look into the mirror and see a weak empathic woman who is controlled more by her emotions than reason. Helga, it is your inner self speaking, you must be stronger. You must jump into survival mode. You must be a fighter like Olga and live to tell your story. I look in the mirror and I smile. "Thank you for refusing my energies."

I walk into Boumer's office without knocking and the first thing spewing out of his mouth is that I am late for work. Next, he lectures me on the dangers of spying on the Wehrmacht while they are doing their jobs.

Really, they reported me already, bastards.

"Herr Boumer, I was not spying on them. Yes, I did see them commit atrocities against a Jewish family. They saw me standing there."

"Yes, they did see you standing there. They know who you are. You are famous in the Third Reich my dear."

"Well, Boumer I do not want that type of popularity, thank you very much!"

"I understand Fraulein but do not let it happen again as you may find yourself being interrogated by the Gestapo. Do you understand? Don't be late for work anymore as it does not look good to the other workers."

"Yes." I respond with a disgusted tone in my voice. I have had enough of his Nazi nonsense. It is my turn to stand up for myself.

"Herr Boumer, for your information as you are aware my mode of transportation is not a comfortable chauffer driven sedan with warm heat soothing my body. I own a bicycle which has seen better days. Each of my tires are fifty percent eroded and I have to deal with the snow and mud sticking to the rim. This makes my bicycle ride more uneven and I frequently have to stop and chip the snow and mud from the rim. Even if I leave my home early to make it to work on time, I am at the mercy of the elements. Do you have a solution? Oh, by the way, the Nazis have confiscated most of the bicycles for their own selfish use."

I fold my arms across my chest and glare at him like my eyes are being blinded by a bright light. The silence is deafening and uneasy but I hold my ground. My heart is not racing, my breathing is calm. I am at peace with myself.

"My Fraulein Helga, you are a very strong woman and your words speak volumes. I wish my wife had such determination and self-respect. I find you very enticing. Now my dear, let's talk about your work here at the registry. I have watched you handle the Jews at the front counter. You are a good Dutch woman as you appease them with your Jewish language skills. Your empathy towards them is not in the best interest of the Third Reich."

I step in before he can spew more venom. "Herr Boumer, what do you suggest that I do. I am an empathic woman and I can't turn off a dominate part of who I am. You have to realize that my empathy ensures that I translate their information correctly. Do you want the Third Reich to be inundated with false information?"

"My Helga, are you sure that you are not German?"

"Boumer, you have checked my lineage and you know that I am Dutch."

"MY Helga, I know that your analytical and language skills are invaluable to the Third Reich. I am also aware that your colleague Leos has limited Jew skills which she gets by with. I know that you want to use your impeccable skills in the special project room. Ared and I are meeting in two days to discuss the efficiently of the registry process and he will hear any recommendations I put forth. I will recommend that you join the workers in the special projects room and stress that you want to use your skills for the betterment of the Third Reich."

Little does he know that I want access to that room to find out what the hell the Nazis are up to!

"Now Helga, give me a kiss and go join your colleague Leos. I will also find a solution to your bicycle woes."

I give him a quick kiss and open the door. I walk out of his stuffy room and walk into a more relaxed welcoming atmosphere. Leos must have told the women what I experienced. I smile and nod my head in approval and join Leos working through the long line of people waiting to be processed.

CHAPTER TWENTY-THREE

Earlier this week, the Nazis instructed the Dutch population to relinquish their radios or suffer the usual consequences. I know that my household will not be one of the lambs appeasing the Nazi wolves. The Nazis have given us until midnight tonight to hand in any radios at their designated collection site. I know exactly what will happen. You do not just drop off your radio and go on your merry way. The Nazis will document your identity and type of radio(s). The Nazis are very thorough on their paperwork and I know that a copy of this list will end up in Berlin. I do not want to be kept in the dark when a war is raging in my city and country.

Mother gets herself into a tizzy over any Nazi orders. She insists that Father hand over the radio for the sake of our family RIGHT NOW. Father continuously reassures her, since the order was issued, that he will hand in the radio. Yet, the clock hands are inching toward the deadline and Mother is aware that the radio is still in the house.

"Lars, you have to get that radio out of here now or the Nazis will look for us."

"Berta, I will take the radio back tonight. Can't you see that I have my coat folded over the kitchen table chair?"

"Yes, I do. Thank you, Lars. I don't want any trouble with the Nazis."

"I know Berta, all of us must abide by their rules."

"Thank you, Father, for defusing that bomb," I silently say to myself.

Father escorts Mother up to their bedroom and I know that he will be back down when she is asleep. It is pathetic that Father is her security blanket. Why am I such a strong woman and she is so weak? Once Mother is asleep, Father descends the stairs lightly as he does not want the creaks to wake her up. He joins the rest of the gang in the parlor for our 'private talk'.

"Father, the radio is our lifeline to what is happening in our country and with the war. The Nazis propaganda machine is ruthless and once our radios are gone, they will bombard our newspapers and nail posters to anything that is vertical."

"You are correct Helga. Lukasz will set up the radio to be tuned into Radio Oranje on the BBC European Services; this station provides us with updates on current affairs and it broadcasts our Queen's regular speeches. Lukasz, I will go outside as if I am returning the radio. I will start my car and turn it off just in case Berta is a light sleeper tonight. I will walk to your cabin and you can hide the radio for us. Lukasz and Olga, I leave it up to you two where you want to set up the radio to listen to broadcasts. You all must realize that I don't like being deceitful to Berta, but the less she knows the better off we are."

CHAPTER TWENTY-FOUR

The Nazis have announced that all Dutch Jews must register at the Central Registry. All non-Dutch Jews are to register at the Central Office of Jewish Immigration which is located within walking distance from our building. I have heard that the Immigration office is infested with Nazi collaborators. One rumor is that these collaborators will track down Jews and arrest them. A second rumor is that Herr Ared has placed a 7.50 guilders bounty on each Jew that is caught. I can't get wound up with all the rumors circulating these days or I will go crazy.

Leos and I agree that when any non-Dutch Jews arrives at our counter, we will process the paperwork as 'Dutch' Jew and alter the information on their cards. I know that this is a temporary fix for these people, but it can buy them time find a safe hiding place.

The line snakes around the building like a green anaconda cautiously looking out for a stalking tiger to pounce on it. In this situation it is the Wehrmacht soldiers who pounce on the defenseless Jews for amusement. There is a window by the registry counter where we can observe what is going on outside. I watch a young violent Wehrmacht soldier torture an older Jewish man. This particular man lowers himself to the cold snow-covered ground and stretches his legs out. The young soldier yells obscenities at the old man and stomps on his right leg and snaps it like an old dried out twig. The man is screaming in agony and his wife is screaming at the soldier. Another soldier stands over the couple and shoots them both in the head. Blood splatters everywhere! Why is God making me a witness of this and other atrocities? I initially plan to go to the census cards filing cabinet and retrieve several cards and then go back to the front counter to help a Jewish family. Instead, an invisible force lures me to the window to witness this atrocity. I wonder if this is my new routine.

The Jewish family at the counter also witness the murder of the older couple. She covers her children's eyes so they do not witness the murder. She is in tears and her husband is consoling her. This family are Dutch Jews. I whisper to them to get out of Amsterdam and save themselves as it is very dangerous for Jewish people. They smile, nod and thank me. I know that they will relay my words to other Jewish families.

I look over at Leos and she is very busy helping another Jewish person. Her Yiddish is not fluent, and I can see that both she and the Jewish person are both getting frustrated at their inability to communicate efficiently. After that person leaves, she takes a deep breath.

"Helga, I want to introduce you to some of my friends, including a wonderful calligrapher," she whispers to me.

I stop what I am doing and ask her the calligrapher's name.

"Leike." Leos responds, "And she is more than a friend."

I am stunned but not surprised as Leike is a very sensual lesbian.

"Leos, I am sorry, but I can't meet tonight." I whisper in her ear. I wonder to myself if they are up to something.

Just before the end of my shift, Boumer sticks his head into the front area and tells me to join him in his office. He is in a jovial mood and I wonder what he is up to. I am getting very suspicious of everyone these days. When I go into his office, he closes the door behind me and puts his arms around me.

"Helga, my love, I have solved your transportation problem."

"Herr Boumer, have you bought me a car?" I comment jokingly.

"My Helga, you have such a wonderful imagination. No, I have a new bicycle for you."

"Thank you, Herr Boumer, does it have a basket for me to put my purse in it?"

"My Helga, the basket is big enough for me to fit in." He says laughing. "And it is a beautiful light blue in color."

"Thank you, how can I repay you Boumer?"

"Well, give me a big kiss."

I give him an average kiss and go back to work at the counter. Leos asks me why I am so happy and I tell her what Herr Boumer gave me. She rolls her eyes and gives me a silly smirk. I grab her left arm.

"Leos, it is called survival and I will take what I can from the Third Reich. They have stolen from each one of us and our country."

"Good night Helga and be safe." She says as she plants a quick kiss on my cheek and leaves.

I am mentally and physically exhausted at the end of the day. I ride my new bike home and am happy that my body is no longer severely impacted by the mounds of ice and snow and the crevasses on my ride home. It is a clear dark night and I stop to admire the full moon and the sparkling stars dancing in the black curtain. I stop at the spot where the innocent Jewish family was tortured earlier this week. Any evidence of their existence has been erased by the blowing snow. Even the sturdy pine tree has freed the child's remains from its hard-unforgiving bark.

I stand at my shiny bicycle and I whisper a Yiddish prayer to this family. "I promise I will never forget you and I will never forget the murders' faces. I will avenge your deaths!

Our house is quiet when I arrive home. Olga usually greets me at the front door, but she is conspicuously absent. I quickly gobble down my cold dinner as if it is my last meal, I climb the stairs and collapse on my bed.

CHAPTER TWENTY-FIVE

I t has been a another busy and heart wrenching day at the registry. I look at the Jewish people at the counter and I want to destroy their cards so they don't exist on paper in the Netherlands. Yet, I know that Berlin will use their records or local collaborators to hunt them down like defenseless animals.

Karl greets me inside the foyer with hugs and kisses when I get home.

"Karl, this is such a surprise."

"Hi baby, I miss you and I want to brighten whatever is left of your day."

"Karl, you are my spark of light in the darkest day."

"Helga, I have prepared a late dinner tonight so that we can talk while enjoying a meal together."

"What about Mother, is she going to join us?"

"She will join us later for wine in the parlor. She is busy modifying clothes to fit her shrinking figure.

This should be interesting my internal voice says to me. At the dinner table where Olga and Lukasz join us, there is the usual light pleasantries with each of us sharing things about our day. I guess we do that to make sure everyone is at ease. Karl is the first person to speak, seriously.

"Helga, I must tell you something important. My real name is Vladimer Swazinko."

"Karl, that is a bit of a surprise, but I had wondered why both of your parents are Russian, yet you are called Karl."

"Helga, my parents changed my name when I was very little. Father told me that it was done to keep me safe from the anti-communist feelings back then. If I used my Russian name to get into medical school, I knew that my application would be sitting on the rejection pile. All of my identification, that I know of lists my name as Karl Swanko, but I don't know what the Nazis have access to. Olga is working on changing my identity."

"Helga," Olga interrupts and whispers, "Karl, Lukasz and I are part of a communist resistance group."

Karl looks at me and puts my hands in his. "Helga will you join us?"

"Yes, of course I will darling. I will follow you to the moon if I have to."

Everyone laughs.

"I knew that you would join us. The communist party has an event planned but it is being kept secret. We need to protect all our identities in case we are interrogated by the Gestapo. There are alternatives to revealing identities and that is a cyanide capsule. I want everyone to have a capsule on them at all times hidden in our garments. I will get Berta to create tiny undetectable hiding spots in our clothing."

Karl whispers that we are going to focus on hiding people and smuggling them out of the Netherlands to Switzerland.

"Are we putting our family in danger?"

"No Helga, but we are in danger anyways just sitting around not doing anything." Lukasz replies.

I direct my conversation at the three of them.

"I know that the Nazis are up to something sinister in the 'secret room'. Census cards are removed from the table and go into the room and then return and are placed in an envelope for Berlin."

"Helga, you have access to powerful information at the registry. The Nazis want to have control over everyone. We need blank census and identification cards. I will give Olga a list of the names of individuals who have died at the hospital. Olga will give you a few names at a time and I want you to steal their census cards. Olga can work on creating new identities. She will need you to assist in the printing of names and signatures. The first people to get new census and identification cards are going to be me and your family. We do not have any of our birth certificates".

"Wait, Karl, father retrieved our important documents when he emptied our two deposit boxes."

"No Helga, he did not. The Nazis have pilfered all of the deposit boxes. When your father arrived there, the boxes were nonexistent. They took the expensive jewelry your mother was storing. The Dutch banker was not able to retrieve the deposit boxes before the Nazis helped themselves."

"Your father revealed all this to me." Olga interjects. "He was only able to withdraw a portion of the money in his bank account. The rest is for the Third Reich."

"Mother will be mortified that her jewelry is gone. That is her contribution to the household when money gets low. She wanted to barter the jewelry to buy food or other supplies. How are we going to survive?"

At that moment, Karl takes four medical bottles out of his inner pocket. "This my love is how are all going to survive. Medication will be worth a lot of money on the black market."

"Karl, how are you getting the medication out of the hospital? Aren't the Nazis and their collaborators watching you?" Olga asks.

"Olga, I thought you had better faith in me. What I do is I go into the medication room and take small amounts of medication every day. When I hear the Germans talking about confiscating specific medications, I sneak into the medication room when nobody is looking and switch the good valuable medication for another drug. I have a nice collection of essential medications. On my next shift I will grab insulin and surgical supplies. Just to make it clear, I don't jeopardize my Dutch and undesirable patients as I give them the correct medications. The German patients are another story, they don't deserve quality care and I do not want to waste precious medication on them."

"Karl don't get caught. Won't the Nazi doctors be suspicious?"

"No, they aren't Helga as they know that we are running short of medications and I haven't given them a reason, yet, to not trust me."

"Is Father aware of what you are doing?"

"No Helga, I keep him out of it for various reasons. Please don't ask any more questions, my love."

"I would like to change the subject. Karl, Leos, my colleague at the Registry is up to something as she is also stealing cards. She wants me to meet her and introduce me to some of her friends."

"Helga, listen to me. Do not associate with this woman outside of work! Keep your distance from her. My contacts have told me that she is under Gestapo surveillance and they want to catch her in the act."

Karl is staying the night in the spare room, but he will sneak into snuggle with me once my mother is asleep. We act like we are teenagers in love. My mind is still saturated with all the conversations tonight. Lots to digest.

CHAPTER TWENTY-SIX

My head is still spinning from last night's discussions. Life is getting more complicated and dangerous as the occupation progresses. Today, I ride to the registry on my new bike. I am sure it was confiscated from a Jewish family. I feel guilt and shame, but I must accept what the enemy gives me. When I arrive at the Registry the Nazis have erected two barricades to control the Jewish people waiting in line. They aren't wild boars you Nazi pigs, I think to myself. I look around the edge of the building and see that the Nazis have deployed NSB thugs to enforce order and control of these people. I know though that they are the ones that really need to be controlled.

Two young Wehrmacht soldiers allow me into the building. There are four of them that rotate guarding and controlling this entrance of the Registry. These young men know me very well and I don't have to show my identification anymore. I arrive early today and hope this does not raise any eyebrows or suspicions. I told mother about these young men and she is making four beautiful silk scarfs for their wives or girlfriends. I know that these scarves will go a long way in manipulating these unsuspecting soldiers.

I climb the stairs praying that I will be able to get the blank census and identification cards and my family's census cards. I am the only worker at the registry except for Boumer, so it is possible. I know that I can justify my early arrival on the efficiency of tires on my new bike. I grab the inkpad and bottle for ink from the front counter. I am not overly worried as it sounds like Leos is in the Gestapo's radar! Boumer's office door is open but he is not in his office. That means he is lurking around somewhere.

Herr Boumer has already opened the filing cabinets and this saves me a lot of aggravation. I quietly and quickly grab Karl, Olga, Lukasz, Mother, Father and my census cards. I close the filing cabinet drawer quietly and place the cards deep in my jacket pocket. I jump in surprise as I see Boumer leaving the secret room. He looks surprised to see me in so early.

"Herr Boumer, good morning. I am alarmed that the filing cabinets are unlocked as they are usually locked at night. Did someone break into the building last night?"

"My Helga, you are such a concerned and observant woman. I must add that you are also very sexy and smart. You are correct that the filing cabinets are open. We no longer lock them at night as there is a double shift of workers working in the coding room."

Coding room. Did he slip that in purposely to see my reaction?

"What do you mean coding room Herr Boumer?" I ask. "I know that the coding room utilizes the information on the duplicate census cards as I see the piles disappear and then reappear to be sent to Berlin every day."

"Fraulein, I am very impressed. Come into my office and tell me what else you observe."

Now, I have to carefully choose my words. "Herr Boumer, would you please excuse me for a moment as I have to go to the lavatory?"

I grab my purse and go into the middle stall. I take our census cards and place them in my sanitary towel boxes. No man in his right mind will rummage through that box. It is taboo. I chuckle and urinate as I fold the cards into the boxes. I go back to his office and am greeted with sweets and coffee on his meeting table. Did he just snap his fingers and these items appear?

"Herr Boumer, are you magical? Do you snap your fingers and coffee and sweets appear out of thin air? You are spoiling me. You will make me too fat for my clothes," I say flirtatiously.

"My Helga, you know that I will do anything for you," he says as he walks over to me and puts his arms around my waist, feeling my curves. "My Helga, you are perfect the way you are."

"Thank you, my love," I reply as I escape his embrace and sit at the meeting table. I pour us both a cup of coffee as he joins me.

"Herr Boumer, I notice that the individuals in the coding room are kept separate from the rest of us. There is one woman who retrieves and returns the census cards sitting on the back table. Also, there are only two of us working out front updating and issuing new census cards, updating existing cards, and issuing identification cards. The lineup of Jews to register themselves is endless. I am worried that this will create a backlog for the coding room. Leos and I can only process so many individuals in one day. I am afraid that this backlog will grow and Ared will report this inefficiency to the Fuhrer."

"Darling, what do you recommend?"

"I recommend that you move two of the women in the back to the front counter. I am unaware of their roles, but I question if their time could be better utilized at the front counter. I know that it may be crowded for four workers at the front counter, but it will speed up the process. There is a lot of cross checking that must be done to ensure that the Jews are providing us with truthful information. I am not sure on the language skills of the other workers. Leos is not fluent in Yiddish, in fact, she is very effective in annoying any Jew she is helping because she takes so long to complete the paperwork."

"Helga, you are very intuitive. I better watch my job and my ass around you. You might want my job!"

"Herr Boumer, I do not want your job. No thank you. But your ass, that is another story mmm!"

"Well for your information, Ms. Sensuous Helga, you can have my ass as long as I can have yours!"

"Of course, Herr Boumer," I say as I caress my bottom in front of him. I look at the front of his pants and a see a small wet spot. I chuckle to myself. I have him wrapped right around my baby finger.

"Well Fraulein, for your information I have two individuals waiting to take over the front desk duties. They are German and can speak a few languages. They don't speak Jew but that is fine by me. I don't want the filthy Jews to breeze through this process!"

"What do you mean two other people? Am I being replaced by a German?"

"My Helga, do not fret as I will always take care of you."

"I know Herr Boumer and I appreciate it," I reply as I grab a couple of treats, give him a kiss and head out to the front.

The workers are starting to trickle in. I hate pointing Leos errors out to Herr Boumer but I need to keep under the Nazis radar. When I get to the front counter, Leos is upset that the ink pad and bottle of ink are missing. I suggest to her that she ask Herr Boumer for another one. I know what I suggest is unethical as I know that will raise more suspicion with Leos, but better her than me. I purposely walk back to the filing cabinets more times than usual and make a point of bending down at the filing cabinets, right in view of Herr Boumer sitting at his desk. I look into his office and see he is smiling at me. How can these other workers not realize that Herr Boumer has a thing for me? Or are they just ignoring it? Ever since I passed the Gestapo test months ago, they have become more friendly, but parts of the iceberg still exist in their demeanor. I pop my head into his office and instruct him to get more treats and coffee for the other workers. I laugh as he jumps up from his desk and grabs sweets from his stash. After work, Boumer wants to give me a ride home, but I remind him that I have my new bike to ride home.

Once I arrive home, I give Olga all the items I have taken from the registry. She secures them in her hiding spot as one never knows when the Gestapo will come knocking. Father is home for dinner and I look at him in disgust. He doesn't talk much about his shifts at the hospital. What is he hiding? After what Olga told me about the safety deposit boxes and his lack of balls to tell us about it, I have lost all my respect for him.

Once Father and Mother have gone to bed, which seems like it takes forever, I go into Olga's room and ask if I can help with the resistance work. She chuckles at me.

"Helga, please pull the census cards for the people on this list; they are from Karl. Also, keep bringing home blank census and identification cards."

"Olga, I stole the ink pad and ink and I know that Leos will be blamed for it."

"Helga, do not feel guilty. You already know that she is under Gestapo surveillance."

I give her a kiss on the cheek and off to bed I go.

CHAPTER TWENTY-SEVEN

I t is a crisp clear Amsterdam morning; the days are getting longer, and I love the warm feeling of the sun on my skin and its rays penetrating my clothes. When I arrive at the registry today, there are about 40 extra Wehrmacht and NSB soldiers outside the registry. I feel their eyes penetrating my soul as I lock my bike to a post. I walk up to the usual guards and they ask me for my identification and search my purse. I ask them if I have to endure this every time I arrive to do work for the Third Reich.

"Yes Fraulein, new protocol."

I climb the stairs and I'm not sure what I will be greeted with. The back room is busy as a beehive. There is a gestapo officer in Boumer's office with one of the workers. An SS officer instructs me to take off my coat and sit down. My turn is next.

"My turn for what?" I ask out loud only to have my words fall on deaf ears.

My colleague leaves the office looking frazzled. Oh shit!

"Fraulein, you can go in now."

I am directed to sit in the chair in the middle of the room and Boumer and the Gestapo agent face me. They don't say anything; they just stare at me. I focus on my breathing to keep me calm.

I look at them and comment, "If you are just going to sit there and stare at me, I have work to do for the Third Reich."

The Gestapo agent walks over to me and slaps me across the face. "You will speak when WE tell you to!"

I am bombarded with questions about the ice cream shop. Do I know the owners? What are their names? Did I know they were hiding Jews with false identification cards? The Gestapo agent stops quizzing me so now I can talk, I think.

I am honest and tell them that I frequent the shop and know their names but I am not aware of them hiding any Jews. Boumer now informs me that yesterday, the owners of the ice cream shop set up a device that sprayed ammonia on two Wehrmacht soldiers and one Officer.

"Oh, my goodness, how are they?"

"That is none of your concern Fraulein! Now what do you know about false census cards and identification cards?"

I firmly tell them both of them that I do not know anything about altered cards. "You can check my work. I am a committed to the Third Reich."

"Fraulein, Herr Boumer and I have checked your work and it is all in order. You see we know who completes specific cards as Herr Boumer's secretary types a list for us. It is another safeguard against terrorist activities. Now, do you have any questions?"

"Yes, what will happen to the ice cream shop owners and the Jews?"

"Good question, the two owners have been interrogated by the Gestapo and they will be executed at the far wall this afternoon. As for the Jews, it is amazing how parents will talk when their children are being tortured. These criminals will also be executed with the ice cream shop owners. Herr Ared is furious! Last night he sent NSB and Wehrmacht soldiers to round up 400 Jewish men 20-25 years of age. These men were taken from their homes in the middle of the night and will be watching the executions as we pile them into the courtyard. Then they will be shipped to a camp in Germany."

An SS officer enters the office and after the Heil Hitler crap hands me a list of handwritten names with addresses and check marks beside them.

"Fraulein, these will be our guests this afternoon. If any of these Jews start causing trouble he or she will be shot in the head. So, I don't advise you to update their census cards yet." The Gestapo agent spews with a callus grin on his face. "That is all Fraulein, Herr Boumer will come get you to watch the show. Heil Hitler."

I return the salute and leave Boumer's office. As I walk out of the door I hear the agent say, "Fraulein, we will round up all the Jews in Amsterdam until they are extinct!"

Leos is next to go into the office and I warn her to be careful. I don't see Leos for the rest of the day. A few hours after I return to the front desk Boumer orders the soldiers to kick all the people in line out of the registry. The doors are shut and locked and I am escorted to a window where the other workers are standing.

"Ladies, it is execution time!" Boumer exclaims.

I look at Boumer in disgust and think to myself, "*I will get even you nasty man!*"

At the end of the day, Boumer informs me that he wants to meet me at 0700 tomorrow morning. I wonder what that is all about? Am I going to go missing also?

At dinner I tell Olga, Lukasz, Karl, and Mother about how every colleague was interrogated and Leos had disappeared. I shared how all of us were forced to watch the executions. Another atrocity that God had me witness! Mother's only comment to me is that I have to be careful. I am surprised that she is not crawling up the walls. Olga must have given her some medication.

Karl speaks to me, "Helga aren't you glad that you did not associate with her and her group?"

The round table agree that I should keep my head down for a little while and don't make any waves. When the time is right, I can instigate a tsunami!

CHAPTER TWENTY-EIGHT

The citizens of Amsterdam have retaliated against the treatment of Jews. Today, the outlawed communist party has organized a massive strike in Amsterdam. The tram, stores, trains and government buildings are all closed. Thousands of people are taking to the street taunting the Germans. Everything is at a standstill.

Karl instructs me to not attend the strike and under no circumstances be a by-stander to this. If I get caught anywhere in the vicinity of this crowd of protesters, it can blow my cover and jeopardize my valuable position at the registry.

"Helga do not go into work. If your boss wants you to work at the registry tell him to pick you up in his car as it is not safe bicycling in public."

Karl is sitting beside me at the kitchen table when Herr Boumer telephones me. He advises me to stay at home until the strike is over. He leaks to me that Herr Ared is furious that the Dutch are so pro Jew. He will make more work for us as there will be arrests, executions, and at least 350 more Jews will disappear, gone from Amsterdam for good.

We both chuckle and I reply, "It's about time we exterminate the rats."

Karl looks at me in disgust after I make the comment. "Helga, that was uncalled for!"

"Karl, I have to play the part. My work at the registry is part of a resistance play and I am just following my lines."

"You are a clever girl. That is one reason why I love you so much. Your sarcasm is impeccable. Now let's spend time with Olga and work on more identity cards."

Olga is continuing to process new cards and identities in her bedroom. We each take a piece of the project like a jigsaw puzzle trying to fit the piece into the full picture. I am given the chore of working on their birth certificates, then transferring this information onto new census and identification cards.

Olga and Lukasz are now Ilse and Gunter Werner and both from different villages along the Russian/German border. The location of these little villages can justify their accents. We work on more false identifications as Karl figures we should start hiding people and get them out of The Netherlands sooner than later. After several hours of working with Olga, Karl and I go into his room. I confess to him that I no longer severely react to the arrests of Dutch men and women and Jews, I just want to get people out of our country quickly and safely.

"Helga, you now have a healthy state of mind. We will get people out of this country, I promise."

CHAPTER TWENTY-NINE

Today when I arrive at work, two of my favorite Wehrmacht soldiers are at their post guarding the entrance of the registry. I walk up to them and tell them that I have a gift for each one of them. Mother has made all four of these men silk scarfs for their girlfriends or wives. She has wrapped each of the scarfs securely in an old newspaper. I hand a package to each of them and they look at me in surprise.

"These scarfs are handmade by my mother. They are for your girlfriends or wives. If you have an extra girlfriend let me know and I will get mother to make a different scarf for them."

"Fraulein, these are beautiful. We do not have extra Frauleins in our lives."

"Excuse me, my handsome soldiers, have you heard anything about my colleague Leos"?

"Fraulein, you did not hear it from us, but she is in Gestapo custody and they intend to bring her over to the registry today to intimidate the rest of you."

"They can try to intimidate me all they want. I haven't done anything wrong!"

"We know Fraulein. When the Gestapo was investigating you, we spoke of our high regard for you."

"Thank you," I say as each of them gives me a kiss on my cheek and then open the gates to hell for me.

When I arrive at the front counter I see the list the SS officer had yesterday sitting there. I take another look at the list and see that twenty men have been shot and the rest are destined for Buchenwald Camp in Germany.

"Girl, don't overreact. Be calm." I tell myself.

Herr Boumer comes out of his office and instructs me to leave the list there. It will be extra work for Anna and Ilse to work on. Who the hell are these women? More fucking Nazi spies reporting to Boumer and / or the Gestapo? Herr Boumer puts his arm around me and escorts me to his office.

"Fraulein Helga, we (myself and Herr Ared) agree that you have proven your commitment to the Third Reich. We don't want you to waste your skills anymore at the front counter. We want you to work in the coding room. Before you say anything, the new Frauleins will be working at the front counter. Their Jews skills aren't the best but we, the Third Reich, have plans for them anyways."

I am elated with the news as this is exactly what I wanted to hear. Herr Boumer grabs my waist and pulls me closer to him. "My gosh Helga, you smell amazing. I want you. I want to devour you."

I put my arms around his neck and we embrace in a sensuous kiss. I place his hand on my bottom and push myself toward him. I can feel his erection against me. He places my hand on his huge erection and I gently stroke the bulge in his pants. It does not take long for a wet spot to appear, like magic!

"Herr Boumer, please hold me tight. Protect me my love."

"Fraulein, I will forever."

As we hug each other I plaster a sinister grin on my face. I tell myself that I will devour and destroy him.

"Fraulein, before I take you to your new assignment, there are important documents for you to sign. The first one is the Aryan Certificate which states that you do not have any Jewish blood in your lineage."

"Herr Boumer, you know that I do not have Jewish blood as you have personally researched me when I started working at the registry."

"Yes, I know my Helga, but this paperwork is a formality and a copy of it will be sent to Berlin. The second document is a confidentiality statement, this means that you will not speak to anyone about what is occurring in the coding room. If you break this confidentiality statement, you and your family will be apprehended and interrogated by the Gestapo. I will not be able to protect you if this occurs. Do you understand?"

"Yes, I do Herr Boumer."

"Also, if you do not accept this position, you will no longer be working at the registry. You will be escorted by the SS to their Amsterdam headquarters, where you will be held and dealt with accordingly. It is a privilege to work in the coding room."

"Herr Boumer give me the papers to sign so I can get on with my life. Have you informed the other workers about my transfer to the coding room?"

"I will do that this morning when Anna and Ilse arrive."

"I think you should get treats out for the announcement."

"You are right Helga; can you organize two large plates of sweets?"

"Doff I think we should also do up a tray of sweets for the coding room workers."

He nods his head in agreement and I get busy organizing German cookies and pastries and Belgium chocolate on three trays. I set the three trays on his meeting table. It is difficult to work with Herr Boumer rubbing the front of his pants against my ass. I keep telling myself all for the resistance.

"My god Helga, you smell amazing. I want to devour you. I am ready for you!" He says as he grabs the front of his pants.

"Herr Boumer, must I remind you that I do not get involved with married men."

He takes my hand, "Now you will meet your new colleagues."

We leave his office and walk to the coding room door. He knocks on it; one loud, one soft, followed by two more loud knocks. The secret knock to get into the room! *Nice security Boumer,* I think to myself. The door opens and blocking the doorway is a tall, broad shouldered woman with piercing blue eyes and a jawline that would make any good Nazi man envious. Heil Hitler!

Boumer and I step into the room and I am immediately transferred to Berlin. All of the women rise from the table and we all do the Hitler salute and squawk "Heil Hitler". It is a Nazi symphony! There are large Nazi flags draping the walls, a huge portrait of Adolf Hitler, a radio squawking German propaganda and music, and an ominous metal machine sitting by itself on a table against the west wall. There is also another door on the south side of the room. I assume this is a 'secret' exit. There is a long table with five other women working with census cards and a long card I have never seen before.

"Fraulein Marie, this is Fraulein Helga, the Dutch woman I was speaking to you about. She is fluent in many languages, including German but her expertise is in writing and speaking Jew. This is an invaluable skill as she will be able to decipher and intercept Jew cards for the Third Reich."

"Fraulein Helga, welcome to the Third Reich's coding room."

I respond with, "Thank you Fraulein." Boumer smiles at me and leaves to return to his office.

"Fraulein, I am your immediate supervisor. I in turn report to Herr Boumer. I will be scrutinizing all of your work. In the beginning I will provide Herr Boumer with daily reports and once I become more comfortable and secure with your work, the reports will be weekly, then monthly etc. Do you understand?"

"Yes, I do."

"This is very important work for the Third Reich and Hitler is counting on all of us to be thorough in our coding."

I nod in agreement, though Hitler is the last person on this planet I want to make happy. I am introduced to the other women and decipher from their accents that three are German and two are Dutch. I am placed between two German women Eva, and Johanna. I set my personal belongings on my chair and take a closer look at the metal monster. It has writing on it in English not German. Interesting.

Marie takes me aside and talks softly to me so we do not interrupt the other women working diligently for the Fuhrer.

"Fraulein Helga, as you can see this machine," as she gently strokes the ice-cold metal, "processes the punch cards that you and the other Frauleins will be coding very quickly. This is very important as this information is used by the local SS and Gestapo to identify and locate individuals based on the data they request."

My heart sinks. This is how they will find people.

"The information on the census card is transferred onto one of these specially designed punch cards. On these cards we can identify if someone is a Jew (code 5), Gypsy (code10), Communist (code 6), not working (code 20), country born (code 30) and so on."

I look at Fraulein Marie and say, "This is a very powerful tool."

"You have no idea Fraulein! Let's say Herr Boumer and Herr Ared want to know where Unemployed Dutch men age 15-45 are living. Individual addresses, place of employment or unemployment, and nationality are standard information that are automatically added to the punch cards. To isolate the criteria we require, we simply change the settings on the machine and feed the Dutch cards into the machine to be processed. As you will see, we keep all the Jewish cards separate, this includes individuals who are not one hundred percent Jewish. Also, if we locate a Jewish name and that person has converted to Christianity, they go in the Jewish pile. Herr Helga, it is a lot of work to keep the census cards and punch cards up to date with information. As you can see, we also have typewriters on our desks to prepare lists of Dutch men aged 15-45 who are unemployed. Well, let's get you working."

I sit on my chair and grab the first census card copy on top of the pile which belongs to a Jewish man. Marie gave me a list of codes to fill in for each criterion and I get at it. I feel sick to my stomach that I am helping the Nazis track people, but I know that I must do my job to learn more.

"Fraulein, today you will work your normal shift. From tomorrow onwards, you will work from 08:00 to 16:00. Do you understand?"

"Yes, I do Fraulein."

"Helga, please call me Marie. We do the formalities only when any of the men come in."

"Marie, can you please get me an after-curfew pass. I need one so I don't get harassed by the Night Demons."

She chuckles and agrees. Hearing a knock on the door she turns. Herr Boumer enters and whispers something to her.

"Alright Frauleins we need to go to the back room as Herr Boumer has several announcements to make."

When we enter, I see all the workers are now standing in there staring at the treats. To be honest, I am eyeing the Belgium chocolate up myself. Herr Boumer makes the announcement of my transfer to the special projects room and the addition of Anna and Ilse to the front desk. Not a word is said about Leos. We all grab some treats and return to the secret room. Marie whispers to me to grab the census card on top of the pile. Marie stands beside me and watches my coding like a wolf waiting to pounce on anything that dares to attack her pups. In this case, the pups are every census and coding card. She watches me complete several cards and then informs me that she will check the rest of my work before the end of my shift.

Near the end of my shift Marie calls me to bring my work to her. I feel like I am in grade school again, but grade school did not have a death sentence attached to it.

"Fraulein, you are a perfectionist. I will see you tomorrow at 08:00 and here is your after-curfew pass. Also, since you will be working in both the back room and the coding room you can leave your personal items wherever you choose."

The temperature has dropped since this morning and the brisk wind cuts through my winter clothing. I will be biking against the wind which will make my ride home long and cold. I pedal quickly to get away from the infestation of Germans that are walking the streets like ladies of the night.

After dinner, Mother goes to bed early. Lukasz, Olga and I meet in the parlor. Lukasz retrieves two bottles of chilled Clio champagne from the kitchen, Olga brings three champagne flutes out and I bring knowledge. I tell them about census cards and the coding machine. They are both surprised that the machine has an English label. We know that the Nazis have to have a system in place to facilitate their systematic roundup of people. Both of them advise me to manipulate our personal census cards as Olga has completed our new identities when it is safe to do so. The last people for me to process are me, Mother, and Father. Lukasz keeps refilling the wine glasses and before we know it's midnight. That does not stop Lukasz from opening the other bottle of Clio. I stay up with my fellow communist resistance members minus Karl. It is agreed that once everyone is comfortable with me and my work in the coding room, I will begin manipulating names for the resistance. After the second bottle, I inform both of them that I have to go to sleep. I try not to slur my words and wobble up the stairs like I am on my old bicycle riding on the rims.

Good night my family!

CHAPTER THIRTY

W hen I arrive at work, I see two black sedans outside the registry. Fuck, what do the Gestapo want now? There are four SS officers lurking at the building entrance. I try to control my body's response to seeing them, but today I am not winning that battle. My breathing becomes labored and my stomach is in a knot. I walk over to the edge of the building and vomit. As I clean myself up, I see the SS officers chuckling at me. I look at them and comment "Haven't you seen a Fraulein vomit before?"

They do not like my comment. They open the building door and push me inside. After pushing me up the stairs they dump my purse on the counter and search my coat and pat me for hidden contraband. One SS officer grabs my identification card and asks me my name, address and date of birth. He then takes my identification card into Boumer's office. A few minutes later he returns and pushes me towards Herr Boumer's office. I scan his office as I enter and see the former Gestapo agent who tried to trick me months back.

"Herr Boumer, what is going on?"

"Fraulein sit here and shut up!"

Now I am very nervous as he never speaks to me that way. Maybe they found out that I stole cards. Fuck! I look at the Gestapo agent smugly and comment "We meet again."

He smiles. "Yes Fraulein, but under different circumstances."

Boumer slams his office door shut, making me jump. The Gestapo agent drills me again on Leos. I have answered all the questions before; I know that they are waiting for me to give the wrong answer.

"Fraulein, why are you shaking?"

"To be honest I get nervous when I am being interrogated about an issue for a second time. I don't like being treated like a criminal."

"Herr Boumer, I see the Fraulein still has her fighting spirit, Fraulein, everyone in this country is a criminal in the Gestapo eyes!"

Boumer agrees like a puppet on a string. The Gestapo agent opens the door and signals to two SS officers to come into the office. They enter, escorting Leos into Herr Boumer's office. Her face does not look human as she is a bloody swollen mess and is having problems walking. Both of the SS officers let go of her and she falls on the floor. They kick her in the ribs and tell her to crawl to the chair in the middle of the room. I want to reach out and help her but Boumer puts his hand on my shoulder roughly.

He whispers in my ear, "Fraulein Helga, do not even think of it or you will end up down there with her, crawling like a worthless animal."

I look at her with empathy and rub my shoulder that Boumer grabbed. I know that she will not survive anymore beatings. I pray she has a cyanide pill to take right away.

"Herr Boumer, why am I part of this interrogation and humiliation?"

"Fraulein we want to show you how we treat a worker who is working for the resistance."

"Fraulein Leos, you have provided us with important names. We will find your lover Leike and deal with her shortly. I think we will try to extract more information from you. I think you will reveal more when we torture your lesbian lover in front of you. Maybe you both should be re-educated about your sexual desires."

By this point Leos has crawled to the chair and is looking up at all of us. She winks at me and smiles. Before the Gestapo agent or SS officers can react, she pinches her left collar and digs out a cyanide tablet. She bites into it and begins to convulse and foam at the mouth. I don't know how the hell she managed to sneak in a cyanide tablet as I am sure that she was strip searched and all of her cavities were searched.

"Fucking whore!" Shouts the Gestapo agent as he kicks her lifeless body with his jack boot.

He storms out of the office as the two SS officers drag her lifeless body out of the building. I am not frightened but angry. Boumer puts his hand gently on my shoulder. I brush him away and go into the coding room. I am worried about my childhood friend Leike, but I have to focus on myself and my resistance group. Leos and Leike are doing the same as me; trying to outwit and subdue the Nazis.

I update Olga and Lukasz on the day's events when I return home. Olga hands me a small list of names from Karl. She firmly instructs me to focus on my task at hand and our resistance group. Do not get emotionally wrapped up in other events. Stay focused! Stay strong!

CHAPTER THIRTY-ONE

Leike

I am getting worried as I have not heard from Leos in several days. Mrs. V. enjoys my company but prefers Ms. Helga's company. I tell Mrs. V. that I will invite Helga over soon. I explain to her that Helga is working at the Central Registry for the Third Reich.

"Leike it is important that you continue living your normal life since the Gestapo is watching the house. Do not engage in any resistance work." She tells me upon seeing a black sedan parked outside of our house.

"I know Mrs. V. I have also seen a black sedan by my photography & calligraphy shop."

Mrs. V. raises her eyebrows and comments that just being alive puts one under their surveillance these days.

I have hidden my underground resistance material, census cards, and identification cards in my basement. Leos is providing me with a large amount of these cards for resistance work. Another thing that I must do is put forth a persona that I am straight. I now have a German boyfriend and he completes my facade. I met him several weeks ago when I was walking to Yvo's flower stall to get Mrs. V. a dozen roses. A young Wehrmacht soldier stopped me and asked me for my identification. I showed it to him, and he asked me where I was going. I told him that I was buying flowers for my aunt.

"Well, a beautiful woman like yourself should not be walking by herself. Let me walk with you and keep you safe."

He walks beside me and we arrive at Mrs. Yvo's flower stall. I ask her for one dozen roses, 10 white and 2 red. She smiles and a few minutes later she has a beautiful boutique of roses ready for me.

"They are beautiful Mrs. Yvo."

"Only the best for my favorite and best customer," she says with a wink.

"How much are they?"

Before she can answer, the Wehrmacht soldier gives her several guiders and tells her to keep the change. I am grateful and cautious. Is he part of the Gestapo ploy to catch me off guard? He walks me to 'my' place and asks me if we can go for dinner the following night. The rest is history and we now see each other all the time. Hans spoils me with flowers, dinners and extra food rations. I have introduced him to Mrs. V. and she has given him her approval.

Lately I have noticed changes in his behavior though. Now when we go for walks, he looks in the direction of the black sedan. Is that a signal? He does not say a word and is more standoffish and our lovemaking sessions are more aggressive. I complain to Hans that he is hurting me but he ignores me and keeps pounding on me until he ejaculates. I ask him what is the matter but he doesn't answer. Finally, I get more than a few meaningless words out of him.

"Leike, I don't know how to tell you this but you are under investigation by the Gestapo. Your lesbian girlfriend, Leos has been interrogated by the Gestapo and she is dead. What do you have to say for yourself?"

"Darling, I co-own a shop where I offer calligraphy services to elite Dutch families and my colleague does portraits for families. Leos was a friend and we were not involved sexually."

"You are a fucking liar!"

"Hans, what the fuck is your problem? You Nazi bastard. Go back to Germany where you belong!" I scream, covering my head in fear that he will strike me, but he doesn't.

"Leike, you are a Dutch whore, and you are not worth my time! I will not associate with a whore like you!"

With that he walks to the front door and slams it as he leaves. I sit on the parlor floor with my head in my hands crying my heart out. Mrs. V. comes downstairs and gives me her hand and helps me up.

"Come here my poor Leike, you do not deserve to be treated that way. Let me get you a warm cloth to wash your face and clean the tears from your pretty face."

"Mrs. V., Leos is dead, and I actually was beginning to like Hans. In the beginning, he was a nice man."

"Leike, war does crazy things to people. You will get over him and find another more suitable man." Mrs. V. looks at me seriously. "We do not know the full extent of what Leos told the Gestapo; I think it is best that you remain in the house. Let's share a bottle of white wine while we make dinner together. Wine always cheers me up."

Together we make a tasty meal using the prime meat and vegetables that Hans brought over yesterday. We indulge in German cookies he also gave us.

"Mrs. V. I am going to miss the extra food that he brought us."

We both smile and devour our dinner.

Before I leave the house in the morning, I ask Mrs. V. to get a note to Mrs. She nods and tells me not to worry with a wink and says, "I am a little old lady minding her own business."

I ride my bicycle to work this morning to work on legitimate projects and to act as if nothing has happened. I see the black sedan by our shop, but I am too busy today with customers to worry about the Gestapo. After work I go to the local bakery and cheese shop to get my rations. Just as I expected they are out of products. Both storeowners give me the same lecture that the Germans are sending most of the food to Germany or they are stuffing their faces. I tell both the shop owners that the Nazis are looking life fat pigs ready for slaughter. We share a good laugh and I leave their shops snorting like a pig! When I get home, empty handed from the shops, I prepare a meager meal consisting of a few potatoes, scraps of meat, and a few carrots. But we still have another bottle of wine! At dinner, after the blessing, Mrs. V. opens up to me.

"Leike, I am tired of the Nazi occupation with the murder of innocent Dutch men and woman and the disintegration of our lives."

"Mrs. V., what are you talking about?"

"Leike, you have many years left. Make wise choices. I am 62 years old. I have lived through the Great War, held my husband when he died in my arms, I have no children, and I am blessed to have you and your friends in my life."

Mrs. V.'s words penetrate my heart. Is she giving up on life?

"Leike, I delivered the message to your friend."

It is decided that in two days Mrs. V. will grab her cane and go for a walk in the park located two blocks from her house. She will have her gray hair wrapped in a warm beige scarf. This is the signal to the resistance person. The code words to be exchanged are: "Nice day for a walk in a park". The answer will be "Too bad we aren't in Brazil." She is unaware of who the member is. That is the way it works with the resistance. I remind her that she must stay in the park like she usually does. That she needs to follow the same routine and to not deviate from it in case she is being watched.

32

MRS. V

The day is finally here for the resistance meeting. I am dressed warmly with a beige scarf and my long fur coat. I walk into the park as planned and am greeted by a young boy. We exchange the code words, and he reaches into his coat pocket and hands me an envelope. I look around to see that nobody is looking and place the envelope in the side pouch of my purse. When I look up, the boy has vanished.

I have always been known as a friendly older lady and I have always greeted fellow walkers in a pleasant manner so I know I have to do the same. Today, two German soldiers walk by and I say good afternoon in Dutch to them. They nod and smile. I know that I cannot scurry back to my house with the envelope as I normally spend time in the park giving sweets, that Leike bartered for on the black market, to children. A mother is walking with two small children and I stop to give each child a candy and whisper to their mother to keep them safe.

I walk slowly to the park exit and notice a sign at the park entrance. The sign states that "Jews are not allowed in the park or to sit on park benches". I am mortified that Jewish children cannot even enjoy a walk in the park like the mother and children I just met. As I turn away from the sign two well-dressed men enter the park. My how handsome those men are, I think. As they walk toward me I say "Guten tag".

The wind is picking up and I don't want to get a chill, so I pick up my pace. I make it home and am happy that I did not get caught. Words are not exchanged between me and Leike but we both know that the meeting was a success, so far.

After dinner we are sitting in the sparsely lit parlor when we hear a couple of taps on the front window. Leike jumps out of her chair and I watch as she instinctively checks her clothes and the blackout curtains for bullet holes. Nope not this time. Leike lifts up the corner of the curtain. She turns and looks and me and tells me its Hans.

"What the hell does he want? He dumped me and called me a Dutch whore. I don't know what to do Mrs. V. Something inside of me is telling me it is not safe, but my heart is overriding any rational feeling I may have."

"Leike," I say, "something is not sitting right with me. Why doesn't he come into my house? It could be a trap."

"Mrs. V. I have to see what he wants. I will just open the door and talk to him while I'm inside."

She opens the front door and sees Hans standing at the bottom of the stairs and he is not alone. He is standing there with two Gestapo agents. She backs into the house.

When she turns around, I am holding my Luger pointed at her head. "Stop, do not move," I say in German.

"What the fuck is going on? Mrs. V. there are two Gestapo agents at the front door."

"Leike, I know. as I ran into them at the park today. Turn around, put your hands up and go outside." I say as I push my gun into the middle of her back.

She looks at Hans and says, "You fucking Nazi!"

"Shut up you fucking spy." Hans says.

A third agent appears with the little boy that I had made the exchange with. "Fraulein is this the boy you met with earlier today?"

"Yes, it is."

The child's eyes are swollen and his head is bloodied. It is evident that he has been beaten. His one leg is smashed and it is dragging behind him. He is whimpering like a wounded puppy.

"Fraulein Leike, do you know this child?"

"No, I don't."

"That is fine as Mrs. V. knows him."

"Mrs. V., why are you doing this? Why have you betrayed me?"

I look Leike straight in the eye. "You have betrayed the Third Reich. You are a Dutch whore with your lesbian lover at the registry, your secret meetings, and your stash of secret documents. How dare you undermine the Third Reich." I walk toward her and spit in her face. ""Fucking whore!"

"All of the information is down in the basement and behind false walls. She is not a smart one as she puts everything in writing. I do believe that her partner at her business was involved in creating false identities. This one is useless to you as she has told me everything. It is amazing how much a bottle of wine loosens lips." I pause and take one last look at her. "Leike don't you know that you are out past curfew."

I pull the trigger and shoot Leike in the head. I laugh uncontrollably as I push her lifeless body down the steps and onto Hans' clean polished boots. I look at the gestapo agent who is holding the shivering and whining boy. I walk down the steps and over to the young boy and shoot him in the head. The blood spatters the Gestapo agent and I watch with glee at the puddle of blood that forms beneath his head. The pool of Leike's blood is expanding in size around her head. I reach down and rub her blood between my fingers.

"Do you gentlemen realize that blood is the lifeline of life. This blood will seep into the ground and feed the earth and the creatures beneath the surface."

The Gestapo agents and Hans look at me like I am crazy.

"Mrs. V. will you take us to where Leike hid the resistance documents?" Hans asks firmly

"You know what Herr Germans. Everything has been moved." Before they can say anything, I yell "Fuck Hitler" I hold the gun to my head and pull the trigger as Hans and the Gestapo look in disbelief.

33

HELGA

The Nazis in Amsterdam are getting more ruthless with the Jews and other undesirables. Every time the resistance avenges the death of individuals at the hands of the Nazis, the Nazis intensify their retaliation. I am working diligently at the registry getting materials needed for new identities.

Karl is over for dinner with most of us, Father is putting in an extra shift for his patients. That is all he told Olga and I don't want to know the details.

"Listen everyone, we know that the Nazis are sending Jews and other undesirables to camps in Germany. I see this information entered onto coding sheets. We need to have a meeting with the Katzes and see about getting them out of Amsterdam and into Switzerland or Spain."

"You are correct Helga; it is time that individuals with new identities be moved out of Amsterdam."

Olga and Lukasz nod in agreement.

"Helga, you and I will visit the Katzes tonight. I know that they can no longer access money in their bank account, but my contacts in the black market are always eager to barter with valuable items." Karl says.

"Karl, could we hide them here?"

Lukasz speaks up and states that he has created a secret room in the attic and a small room underneath the floor in his cabin.

Karl and I excuse ourselves and go to change into dark clothing. Darkness is our best protection against the Nazis. I look up at the sky and it is a very dark night, there is a blanket of clouds blocking the light from the moon and the stars. Perfect night for spy work! Karl and I take the indirect route to the Katz house. We meander around and between the trees, slither behind Lukasz's cabin and eventually end up at the Katze's back door. We knock and Sarah answers and ushers us into the parlor until the Katzes have finished dinner. She brings us each a glass of rich fruity red wine which is smooth on the palate. Mr. & Mrs. Katz join us for a glass of wine.

"Mr. & Mrs. Katz we have come over to talk seriously to you."

I tell them what is happening in the coding room and how the Nazis are rounding up Jews and any person who has defied the Third Reich. Karl mentions that he is connected with people who can get their family and Sarah out of Amsterdam. We both stress that the Germans are engaging in the systematic elimination of the Jewish population.

"Please listen. I have seen the battered bodies."

Mrs. Katz looks surprised, but Mr. Katz is calm, and his blank expression indicates that he is probably analyzing and processing what we just said.

"Thank you, Ms. Helga and Mr. Karl, we are aware of the dangers of the Nazis. Our family has been in this country for centuries and our forefathers have endured turmoil and have survived."

"Mr. Katz, we are offering you an opportunity to escape the Nazi oppression."

"I will not run from the Nazis!" Mr. Katz firmly states.

"Mr. And Mrs. Katz, please think of your daughter and your unborn child."

"What about our paintings, jewelry and other treasures?" Mr. Katz asks.

"You can hide items at our house." I say with confidence. "Mr. Katz, the Nazis take inhabitants from their homes and clean the inside of the house out. They claim all of the house contents. I am sure that these are being shipped to Germany like our food supplies. Please think about it. We will leave you for now but please let us know in the next couple days. Olga, Lukasz, and Berta will be home during the day. Please come to our back door and let them know your response or come over at night when we are home."

CHAPTER THIRTY-FOUR

Three days after our meeting with the Katzes, they both come to our back door. Olga invites them in, and we retire to the parlor. They both look pale and tired as the bags under their eyes are resting on their chins.

"Mr. Karl and Ms. Helga, we thank you for your concern about the safety of our family, but we have decided to stay together; I do not want to separate my family."

"Mr. Katz your family will only be separated for a short period of time. We will move you all though the network. If you want, Mrs. Katz can hide here where we can monitor her pregnancy. If you want, we can hide everyone in Amsterdam until the baby is born. Remember Father is a doctor."

"I understand your concern, but we will not run from the Nazis."

"Mr. Katz don't be so proud! If the Nazis come after you, they will ship you and your family away and confiscate all what you have." Karl says.

"Mr. Karl, they have already stolen my bank accounts and now I am working for a German who runs my company. I must stay, I have employees at my business I must take care of!"

"I understand Mr. Katz but will you reconsider allowing the women in your family to escape?" I plead with him.

"This is a firm NO. I will not have my family separated. This is my final answer! This topic is now closed. Mrs. Katz it is time to go home NOW!"

The Katzes get up to leave and I suggest that we say a Jewish prayer of guidance and protection.

We pray and end the night.

CHAPTER THIRTY-FIVE

Today, the Germans issue an order that all men, both Jews and Christians from the age of 10 years and older are to assemble at the marketplace. Out of the back window in the back office, I watch the Nazis corralling all of these men and boys. If the order is not obeyed, the defiant individuals are to be arrested along with all their family members and sent to prison. In addition, they will lose their house and contents – everything! I watch as the Nazis separate the group into Jews and Christians. Everyone is forced to sit on the cold ground. Two Christians are late, and they are both shot. I watch as the Nazis subdivide the groups again. From what I can see, they have separated the able bodied from the weak and old.

Several of the Christians come into the registry afterwards and tell the workers that the German soldiers searched each person and confiscated everything from the Jews. I am in the back office when these men are speaking to Anna and Ilse. I pour two glasses of water and take them to the men. They tell us how the Germans made them stand for hours and how they were released because they were not viewed as able-bodied.

The Germans load the able-bodied Christian men and boys onto trucks and take them away. The able-bodied Jews are the next ones to be loaded onto trucks. But they are beaten with clubs while they are waiting to be loaded. One man talks of one incident in which a child was forced to beat his father and then vice versa. These two were thrown onto the truck with the able-bodied as the Nazis could still squeeze work out of them. Any man, Christian or Jew, who sat on the ground suffered the consequences of now standing. One of the Wehrmacht soldiers would extend one of his legs out and another soldier would jump on his leg and break it. Then they force that poor man in excruciating pain to stand. If he falls, they will shoot him.

I have one hour left in my shift and I look out the window one last time. The Jewish men and boys are running from the clubs and bayonets of the German soldiers. Some men lay dead or dying while others with their broken legs are beaten to death.

The Nazis have successfully turned the once beautiful square into a collection point for their distorted perspective on the value of life.

A smug SS officer drops off a list and an envelope of identification cards at the front counter. I want those census cards and identity cards. Once the Nazi leaves, I ask Anna if I can borrow the material the SS swine dropped. I look at the list and see that all of the Jewish men and boys were born outside of this country. These are some of the Jews that had to register at the Central Office of Jewish Immigration. The list also indicates that some of these Christian and Jewish boys and men are destined to the Buchenwald and more are destined for Auschwitz. How can I save people from these transports?

I walk into Boumer's office and tell him that we have to talk. I close the door behind me, and he has a dumbfounded look on his face.

"My Helga, I miss you and love you. What can I do for you?" I show him the list that the SS officer dropped off.

"Herr Boumer, the census cards of these individuals have to be checked, updated, and then the information transferred onto the coding sheets. Wouldn't it be more efficient if one person handled the whole process?"

Boumer is sitting in his desk chair looking at me. I can't read his mood. I see that the shutters are closed and hopefully nobody can see in through the cracks. I walk toward his desk and sit on the edge of it with my legs a little apart. Thank goodness I am wearing pants. Then I undo two buttons of my blouse so he can see my brassiere. I undo one more button and lift my brassiere about my ample breasts. My nipples are rigid and monolithic.

"You know Herr Boumer that I am capable of doing that position."

I look at his face and his lustful eyes. They are sparkling like bright stars radiating in the sky on a clear night. I guide his head toward me and place his head between my breasts. He devours my breasts like a savage animal. I lean my head back praying that this humiliation will end soon. He latches onto my left nipple like a famished baby. He is more aggressive than I anticipate and bites my left nipple hard.

I push his mouth and head away and lower my brassiere to protect my sore breasts. "Herr Boumer, you are more aggressive than I imagined. You actually hurt my left nipple as you bit on it too hard."

"I am sorry my love, but I have been waiting for this opportunity since the first time I set my eyes on you."

"What a pathetic man, so weak." I say to myself.

"Herr Boumer, what about my recommendation?"

"Helga, let me talk to Marie."

"Like that?" I say as I point to the wet stain in the front of his crotch.

"Shit, I better wear my jacket!"

I leave his office and his secretary gives me a grin.

"Good one," she says.

She is another one that I have problems reading. Maybe she tells his wife about our little rendezvous' in his office. I smile and walk over to the cabinet and keep working on my previous project. Marie and Boumer go into his office, close the door, and are chatting for quite a while. She opens the door smiling and waves me into his room.

"Fraulein Helga, you never cease to amaze me. Your intellect surpasses the smartest SS officers in the Third Reich. I am going to try to see if I can have you meet our leader. He already knows about you and he is very impressed with your problem-solving skills and your dedication to the Third Reich. I agree with Herr Boumer that the process must be streamlined. You will be responsible for processing this list of names who are destined for Buchwald Camp in Germany. You can finish working on your current cards and will begin working on the list tomorrow. I hope you realize that information on this list follows a person wherever they go. Your accuracy, diligence, work ethics, and commitment to the Third Reich are well noted."

"Thank you, Fraulein Marie and Herr Boumer, for entrusting me to such an important project. I am sure that Berlin would like this list processed right away, but I want to make sure that it is done accurately without any errors."

I stand up and give both the Hitler salute and say, "Heil Hitler".

"Fraulein Helga, since you will be working in both areas, I will make sure that the filing cabinets are open. If not, the keys are located here." Boumer says as he points to his top desk drawer.

"Thank you."

He is not thinking this process out properly. He normally locks his office door and I am sure he locks his desk at night. Am I a magician?

I bicycle home and am torn with what just happened. I am elated with my new project as it will provide me with an opportunity to steal blank census and identification cards and steal the existing cards for the resistance. I arrive home around 22:00. Mother and Father are sound asleep. Olga is awake and has a plate of food for me. She joins me at my informal eating table, my lap, and I tell her about the events of the day and elaborate on how these actions make me feel like a cheap whore.

Olga puts her arms around me and tells me I am not a cheap whore. I am in fact, a beautiful spy who must extract information by any means possible. She always chooses the correct words to make me feel better. Olga informs me then that Mrs. Katz was true to her word and came over to our house earlier. As much as she wants to leave her husband to save herself, Elishva, and Sarah, it is not possible. Her husband insists that they stay together as their family has been a foundation in Amsterdam for over one hundred years.

"Olga, I know that we are disappointed in their decision, but we must respect what they want."

"I agree Helga. But that is not all. Mrs. Katz wants us to hide some of their family heirlooms and assets over at our house. She is the practical one and does not want the Nazis to get their hands on their most valued possessions. This afternoon she, Elishva, and Sarah brought precious items over to Lukasz's cabin. She grabbed me to go into her closet to collect most of her beautiful dresses and her daughter's fancy clothes and give them to Berta. Lukasz has placed the art pieces you like in your room."

"Did you tell Father?"

"No, I didn't and please do not tell Karl either. Make sure you hide those paintings before you go to sleep."

I look at Olga and ask myself what the hell is going on? Keeping secrets from Father and Karl?

Olga must understand what I am thinking. "Trust me Ms. Helga."

I climb the stairs to my bedroom very confused. I obey Olga and hide the paintings in the false wall that Lukasz created. I don't know who to trust!!

36

LARS

Today, I chaired an important meeting in the hospital doctors' lounge. Dr. Karl is standing at the back of the room with his folded arms against his chest. He told me that he hoped to remain invisible to any of the Nazi collaborators in the room. I know that he suspects two of the attendees are Nazi collaborators and he knows there are more, but who are they?

I begin the meeting, "The Nazis expect ALL Dutch Doctors to be members of the Nazi's Doctor' Guild. As we have all witnessed and experienced in this hospital, the Nazis' want us to adhere to their version of care. These Nazi Doctors clearly violate medical ethics. One of my Jewish patients was recovering from a tubal ligation. When I finished my rounds and my shift she was recovering quite well. When I came in the following morning, she was dead. I checked the chart and it said cardiac related. That woman did not have a cardiac issue. She had a healthy heart. Has anyone else experienced the same mysterious deaths?"

Almost every Doctor nods.

"Do you know that our Pathologist is pro-Nazi and will not deviate from what is written on the patient's chart? The disgusting thing is that he is Dutch! I went to medical school with him. I will not take any more of your time today. I will prepare a letter stating that we, Dutch Doctors, will not become part of the Nazis' Doctors Guild. I will leave it on my office desk in a folder for you all to sign. Thank you."

The Doctors file out of the lounge like little soldiers and begin their daily routines

"Lars, we must be careful as the Nazis will seek vengeance on us." Karl states.

"I am aware Karl, but I will not put my patients at risk."

"Lars, how about putting your family at risk? Are you sure you are doing the right thing?" He asks me before leaving the room.

I leave the Doctors' Lounge and head straight to my office. I will type the letter myself as my secretary does not need to be involved. I know that I have engaged in unethical practices providing support to patients who want to commit suicide or have an abortion. This is not the same as the Nazis' Doctor Guild as this was the patient's choice, big difference!

Within a week, the doctors that are going to sign the letter have done so. Karl's signature is suspiciously absent. I place the letter and the attached sheet of signatures in an envelope and walk into the Nazi Hospital Director's office and set it on his desk. Then, I walk out without saying a word. I am smiling as I walk to another of my patients as I know I have done the right thing. I am proud to be a patriotic Dutch doctor!

CHAPTER THIRTY-SEVEN

I t did not take long for the other resistance groups to become aware of what happened to Leos, Mrs. V., Leike, and the little boy. I am sure they are heroes in the resistance world.

A friend told me that several days before the death of the Mrs. V. and Leike, they had seen Mrs. V. visit Yvo's flower stall to buy beautiful flowers for her home. She said that she saw her pass Yvo a small scrap of paper to read.

"I think most people would have thought it was a list of flowers she wanted in her boutique. Yvo did glance at the piece of paper before going into the production area and bringing out an enormous flower bouquet laden with all colors of the rainbow including two red carnations and roses. However, we have discovered that Mrs. V. was feeding the Gestapo false information. We think this is what she was doing. My contact in the resistance found out that Mrs. V reported to the Gestapo that there were forged documents in her basement, and they belonged to Leike. Leike had become a liability and was leaking 'real' information to the Gestapo such as the location of other resistance groups members. She had her dirty hand in getting six resistance members arrested. These individuals are still rotting in a Gestapo cell. We figure that Mrs. V. did her best to discredit Leike but she knew in the end she had to set a trap and execute her! After Leike was shot, the Nazis stormed her shop hoping to find the photographer and his equipment. The Nazis had the shop under surveillance but somehow, he managed to slip away. There was a steady stream of people coming and going from the shop. On several instances they were seen stopping people who had left the shop and demanding to see their photographs. In most of the cases, they were carrying family portraits but, other people had what looked to be legitimate pictures for their identification cards. The photography equipment and supplies were steadily removed from the store in baby prams and under women's skirts. Your gardener Lukasz met these brave Dutch men and women at a disclosed sight on designated days and took the supplies and materials to his cabin. The photographer successfully escaped dressed as an older woman hunched over her cane. He walked right past the Gestapo agent's sedan hunched over taking shuffling baby steps. He is well hidden from the Gestapo!"

"We know that Mrs. V. was fighting for the resistance. Before she died she went into the hospital complaining of chest pains. She was seen by your father. She was seen slipping a piece of paper to your father. We believe it had important information on it."

After hearing this all I approached Father.

"Father, what was on the piece of paper that Mrs. V was seen slipping you at the hospital?"

Father looked at me with a grim look on his face. "I am sorry Helga but I cannot give you that information. It would be too risky. All I can tell you is that there was a name on it. Mrs. V. didn't think this person could be trusted. Please be very careful."

CHAPTER THIRTY-EIGHT

A t 04:00 this morning, I am wakened by the sound of car doors slamming and loud German voices. I jump out of my bed. My heart is racing and my chest is getting tighter as if it has a mind of its own. It feels like a boa constrictor tightening its grip around my chest, squeezing every drop of air out of my lungs! I take slow deep breathes to try to gain control of my breathing and escape the boa constrictor. Relax Helga! While I am trying to adjust my breathing, I look under the blackout curtain and see the silhouette of a sedan and two German officers in their caps. They are standing on the Katz's front lawn. As they walk up to their house, I see another vehicle arrive. Its headlights are on and I see it is a truck carrying soldiers in the back. I know that they have come for the Katz family!

I am hoping and praying that Lukasz heard the commotion out front and was able to quickly get any of the family members out of their home. I know that this is wishful thinking! Mother is also awoken by the noise and both her and Father come into my bedroom. Mother is frantic and orders me to put the curtain back down or before they come over and arrest me. To appease Mother, I do as she asks.

Father puts his arms around mother. "Relax Berta, they are not after us, they are after the Katzes."

"What have the Katzes done? They are hardworking people."

"They're problem is that they are classified as enemies of the Third Reich. They are Jews."

"Well, the Nazis could still come over here."

I give father a stern look.

"Berta don't worry. Let's go back to bed. Helga will keep an eye on the Nazis and will inform us if they come over here, won't you Helga?"

"Yes Father!"

Thank gosh Father is able to defuse her irrationality.

I step lightly down the stairs as I do not want to waken Olga. I grab a chair from our kitchen table and place it by our large parlor window facing the Katzes' house. I feel hands on my shoulders and jump in surprise.

"Sorry to scare you, Helga." Olga says.

"Sorry if we woke you up."

"It's ok, I'm awake now. I will grab a chair and sit on the other side of the window. Hopefully, we won't get caught watching the Master Race destroy a family. Helga, we are witnesses to their atrocities!"

I open the window two centimeters so we can, hopefully, hear the dialogue.

The Nazis have kicked in the Katze's front door and I can hear screaming echoing from the house. I hear Mrs. Katz screaming as they violently push her out the front door and throw her onto their lawn.

"Where is you whore daughter and your slave?" I hear them ask Mrs. Katz

"I don't know!"

"You lying fucking Jew." A gestapo agent screams as he kicks her in her swollen belly. "Maybe your Jew kid will be born with my boot print on its head."

I look over at Olga and she is fighting back tears. I feel my tears flowing down my cheeks, but I am speechless. I look at poor Mrs. Katz holding her belly and crying. I see them drag Mr. Katz out of his house and throw him onto the lawn where they repeatedly kick him in the head and his body. Both of the Katzes are screaming, but their screams fall on deaf ears. Mr. Katz lifts his arm up. One of the Gestapo agents walks over to him. Mr. Katz is saying something to him. Next thing I know two Wehrmacht soldiers grab his arm and drag him back into the house. Mrs. Katz tries to get up from the hard ground and they push her down again.

She is screaming for her husband. The Gestapo agent has had enough and stomps on her head. The screaming stops. Mr. Katz returns, after what seems like forever, with what looks like a gold necklace dangling from his hand. He then puts his hand into his pockets and pulls out other items. I am assuming that they are heirlooms and jewelry that Mrs. Katz did not bring over to our house to hide. I watch as he hands these items to the Gestapo agent and points to his lifeless wife. Mr. Katz drops to his knees and crawls over to his lifeless wife's body. He puts his hand on her swollen belly hoping to feel his unborn child. But the child is gone also. He looks up at the Gestapo agent who has pieces of his wife on his boot. He screams at him in Yiddish! The Gestapo agent laughs in his face and taunts Mr. Katz with the jewelry in his gloved hand. He then raises his gun and shoots him in the head. I cannot process the words clearly. My mind and emotions are overrun with grief, shock, and anger. Tears are silently flowing like lava down a mountain onto my chin.

I turn to Olga and say, "I never knew their first names."

Olga nods and we hug each other and cry on each other's shoulder leaving a salty moist spot on our clothes. As Olga has her arms around me, I begin to recite the Lord's Prayer and she joins in.

"Don't worry Mr. and Mrs. Katz, we will take care of your daughter and Sarah. We will get even and seek revenge on those pigs." Olga whispers.

I hear the Gestapo agent yell, as if he is outside our window, for the soldiers to find the Jew daughter and the housekeeper NOW!

We look under the blackout curtain and watch the fury of activity. One of the soldiers points to our house and we see the Gestapo agent shake his head.

Olga looks at me, "They may come knocking on our door so we must make sure that all of our resistance material is well hidden!"

I hear the creak of the stairs and the heavy stomps of Father as he comes down the stairs with Mother right behind him. Mother and Father sit on the couch in the parlor and ask for an update. I inform them that Mr. & Mrs. Katz and their unborn child are dead. Father is speechless and has a blank look on his face, he reminds me of a blank canvas waiting for an artist to brush color onto it and create a masterpiece. The Nazis could not find their daughter and Sarah and they are like wild animals searching for their prey. Mother is clearly upset and yet, I would expect her to be more irrational. Father must have given her a sedative. I know that she comprehends what is going on. Olga goes over to mother and whispers in her ear. Mother has an out of place smile on her face. I go over and hug her and tell her that I love her. Olga suggests that she makes a pot of tea for everyone and asks me to join her.

"Helga, I must tell you something and you must promise not to tell Karl."

"Alright."

"The other two women are safe and hidden in Lukasz's cabin."

I look in surprise and Olga places her finger on her lips signaling me to be quiet.

We have our tea in the parlor and the silence in the room is deafening. We can hear the soldiers shouting outside. At least they didn't bring their dogs to sniff them out. I tell myself that they are putting in a lot of effort to find two women! Father has to get ready for his shift at the hospital and Mother joins him upstairs. Olga grabs my arm once she is sure that Mother and Father are in their bedroom.

"When Mrs. Katz was bringing items over to Lukasz's cabin to hide, we had a meeting in his cabin. We knew that the Gestapo would come to the front door first. It was planned that at the first sound of trouble, Sarah and Elishva would run out the back door and hide behind the trees and make their way to Lukasz's cabin. They were supposed to hide under the floorboards until it was safe. We knew that they would be taking a chance at getting caught sneaking out the back door, but they had to take it. Mr. Katz died not knowing what had happened to Elishva or Sarah, but that is the way it had to be done. They will come out of hiding once the Germans are done snooping around."

The German soldiers hang around for a couple days combing our back yard for the two women. They pound on our door asking if we have seen the fugitives. Olga informs them she hasn't, but they are welcome to search our house if they choose to. Two of the officers come into the house and do a quick search. They interrupt Mother who is in her dressmaking room. I hear them apologize to her for interrupting her work and ask if they can look in her room. Mother is cooperative and even gives each of the soldiers a silk scarf for their wives or girlfriends. Mother is smart as the scarfs she gives them are in red, white, and black. They do not have swastikas on them, but they have the Nazi colors. They thank mother and leave. Before the door closes Mother firmly tells the soldiers that she and her family do not associate with filthy Jews.

Once they leave, Olga gives Mother a smile. "Nicely played Berta, would you like a drink of Clio?"

"Yes, please and please join me in the parlor. Any Belgium chocolate left?"

"There sure is, Helga's boss is so infatuated with her that he brings her chocolate all the time. I told her next time to ask for pineapple and oranges!"

CHAPTER THIRTY-NINE

Olga tells me to go to work and focus on my job. It is important for me to keep bringing blank cards home. She tells me that me, her and Lukasz will need to have an important resistance talk tonight.

Why not Karl my love? He is a member of the communist resistance. I am sure that Olga has her reasons.

When I go into work the first thing, I do is remove the three Katz census cards and Sarah's. I walk into Boumer's office and tell him that these people are dead! That I have been up since 04:00 watching and listening to the Nazis murder this Jewish family. Even an unborn child is not safe around these savages! Then I burst into tears.

Doff walks over to me and puts his arms tightly around me. "You know that I will protect you my Helga."

I look at him in disbelief and annoyance. "Really Herr Boumer at a time like this you are spewing the same lies to me. I am not in the mood to hear them. I am tired and hungry. Now let me go and complete the file on the Katzes!"

I walk out of his office and turn to see his secretary scurry into his office like a rat looking for morsels of information. I fight back tears as I complete the coding sheets on the Katzes and Sarah. I spend the day in the back office, processing the Jews and whoever else the Nazis have exterminated from our country.

CHAPTER FORTY

I t has been two weeks since Father handed in the letter to the hospital administrator. Father doesn't say anything about any feedback. When Karl visits, I ask him about it, and he says that all is quiet. I know that they are both lying to Mother and me.

After dinner I tug on Father's arm and pull him into our foyer. "Father what the hell is going on. I know that the Nazis will not let that letter go. Will you stop protecting me."

"Helga, my dear. I am sorry for hiding the truth from you. Doctors are disappearing from the hospital. Also, you should know, Karl did not sign the letter!"

"Father, maybe he is afraid of putting me in danger."

"Maybe." He replies as he walks away.

The next morning at work, I look up several doctors' names I know in the census cards. Dr. Dyker is deceased. Dr. Schmidt deceased. Dr. Hiltz deceased. The cull of Dutch doctors has begun. What about Father and Karl? I hope they are safe.

Three days later I receive a frantic call from Mother! "Helga, they have taken Father. I told him to go into hiding but he has always been too proud and stubborn."

"Mother, put Olga on the telephone, please."

"Olga, its Helga, please look after Mother, The Nazis have Father, and I will check with Herr Boumer to help me find him."

"Yes dear, I will take care of your mother. Karl is aware and he is trying his best to get your father released."

After speaking with Mother, my eyes are filled with tears. What have the Nazis done with Father? Why didn't he leave? I walked into Boumer's office crying and shaking.

"Where is my father, my daddy?"

Doff puts his arms around me and does his best to console me.

"Fuck, I hate his war!" I scream at the top of my lungs. I am sure they heard my scream in Berlin!

"Helga, I will contact the Gestapo. Go grab yourself a glass of wine, you look like you could use it!"

His secretary comes into his office with a look of concern on her face. I hand her a glass of wine that I have poured not saying a word. She smiles and stands in Boumer's office waiting for his instructions. I have always thought of her as a wall flower, but she is in fact very intuitive. I pour Doff and I a glass of wine. After what seems like eternity, Boumer informs us that Father is being held by the Gestapo in the local prison where they are interrogating him. He looks at his secretary and asks her to call the Gestapo headquarters to tell them that we are coming over.

Doff sits in the back of his car with his arm around me. He whispers in my ear that things will be alright. I accept his loving gestures with gratitude and place my left hand on his lap. He gives me a gentle kiss on my head. Upon reaching the prison we are asked for our identification and my purse and jacket are searched. The officer also runs his hands over my body checking for contraband. I pass the inspection and we are escorted to where Father is being held.

We find Father in an interrogation room with his hands tied behind his back. His left eye is swollen shut and there is a huge gash across his forehead caked with dried blood. I run over to him and firmly attach my hands and arms around his neck. They will have to pry me away from him. I tell him through my tears that I love him. The guards walk over and unravel my hands and arms from his body. In his parched lips he mouths to me "Don't trust him".

I look at the Gestapo agent and scream, "Why are you doing this to my father? He is an honorable man."

I look over at Father and he tells me that he loves me and then closes his eyes. I watch his chest rise and fall and I can see that his breathing is labored.

"Fraulein, your father has chosen to defy the Third Reich."

"Yes, he has, and you have one little puppet doctor who will do anything you ask!"

Then I turn to my father, raise my arm in the Hitler salute and yell "Heil Hitler". He smiles! I grab the soldier's luger and I shoot Father in the head. Blood splatters on my dress and oozes out of his fatal wound in his forehead.

Doff and the Gestapo agent are surprised at my actions.

"Herr Boumer, I will personally update his record when I return to the registry!"

I turn toward the interrogation room door and ask Boumer if his driver can take me home as I need to wash Father's blood off my face and change my clothes. The ride to my house is quiet. Boumer does not say a word and keeps himself busy by looking out the tinted car window. His heart and soul are as cold as mine are!

I enter our house and Mother and Olga look at me. "Mother, the Nazis murdered Father, he is gone."

I look at Olga with a blank look on my face. Mother comes over to me and puts her arms around me. I put my arms around her and stare off into the distance not focusing on anything. Mother is silent as Father's lifeless body.

"Olga, can you please fix Mother tea. I must clean up and get back to the registry."

Olga puts her arms around Mother and slowly walks her to her favorite chair. She looks frail like a rag doll ready to collapse in half.

When I return to the registry, Boumer has an inquisitive look on his face. He doesn't say a word though. All I want to do is hide myself in the coding room, away from his eyes and his heart. I walk into the coding room and do the Hitler salute and say, "Heil Hitler". Boumer informs all my co-workers, even the coding room workers, while I am in the room about Father's execution. At least he left out the part that I scattered his brains on the interrogation room floor. I am inundated with hugs and thank my colleagues for their kind words. I hope nobody picks up on my sarcastic tone.

The night of Father's death is very emotional for all of us including Karl. Mother wants to give Father a proper burial but I tell her that the Gestapo will not release his body. I tell her that we can say goodbye to Father by maybe planting his favorite flowers in the spring. Mother, accepting the fact that she will never see him again, agrees to this idea. We know he has a favorite spot in the back garden where he liked to smoke his pipe and read one of his favorite books. Karl wants to cuddle and sleep with me but I push him away.

"Karl, you do not want to cuddle with a murderess!" I think to myself.

When I arrive at work the next day, my desk is filled with two beautiful flower bouquets and a wonderful food basket containing exotic fruits one could only dream about. I read the cards and one is from the workers in the back area, one is from the coding room workers, and the beautiful food basket, complete with two bottles of very expensive bubbly wine, is from Doff. I spend the next hour thanking my colleagues and answering questions about how I am doing and how Mother is coping. Finally, I free myself and go into Doff's office.

"Herr Boumer, thank you very much."

"Helga, you are important to the registry and more important to me. Oh, your favorite florist, Mrs. Yvo requested that you drop by and see her. Why don't you do it now Helga, and I will get my secretary to drop these gifts at your home."

"Herr Boumer, please leave one of the bottles of bubbly for us here!"

I put on my coat and walk to Mrs. Yvo's flower stall. How do I tell her that I murdered my father? I won't tell her unless she asks. When I enter the flower market, she jumps off her floating stall and comes running to give me a hug!

"Helga, I heard about your father, I am so sorry. How is your mother doing?"

"She is coping as best as she can. I am sure that Olga is feeding her sedatives like candy to a child."

"Helga, would you like a collection of your favorite flowers in your favorite colors? Come into the preparation room so we can talk in private please."

She takes my hand and leads me into the back room. She then turns to me and says," Helga, Mrs. V. visited your father at the hospital before she died. She handed him this slip of paper. Don't ask me how I got my hands on it but let's say there are nurses and doctors in the hospital who are anti-Nazi."

She hands me the piece of paper and begins to select flowers for my bouquet. She has an array of beautiful flowers that I know are difficult to access. I walk over to Mrs. Yvo and whisper in her ear with a smirk on my face, "Your contacts in the black market are coming through for you."

Yvonne turns to me and blurts, "Bite your tongue young lady. I am a legitimate business owner".

We both smile at each other. She shows me a line of four other arrangements which she has completed and is waiting for them to be picked up. These arrangements all have little swastikas decorating the arrangement. She smiles and tells me that she keeps some of the rose thorns on their stems so hopefully the Nazis will prick themselves and bleed to death! We both agree and I say, "Wishful thinking!"

"Mrs. Yvo, I have something to confess to you."

"Go right ahead dear, I am all ears."

"I shot Father when he was in the Gestapo interrogation room. I grabbed a soldier's gun and shot him in the head. Father wanted me to terminate his life. Before I shot him, he mouthed to me 'Don't trust him'!"

"Helga, do not feel guilty about what you did; it was your father's wish."

"Mrs. Yvo, he never told me why and that is the part that is eating at my heart and soul!"

"Miss Helga, please sit down while I tell you something your father relayed to me. I spoke to your father last week and he suspects that Karl is working for the Nazis. In fact, it is believed he is one of their key collaborators."

I interrupt Mrs. Yvo and look at her in shock. "Fuck, he knows what is going on in my house."

"What is going on in your house Helga?"

I look at Mrs. Yvo and contemplate if I should reveal the secrets which are going on in my home. She detects my uneasiness and whispers to me that she is part of the Communist resistance. She signals me to get out of her chair and looks at me seriously.

"Listen Helga, this is what you must do. You need to keep him out of your house or hide all the resistance material that you have. If I were you, I would not talk to him. I know that he is busy at the hospital doing the Nazis dirty work. Instruct Olga and Lukasz to change their identities. Also, get Olga to throw out any medicines he has brought from the hospital. I suspect they are poisons! Now go back to the registry and call Olga."

"What about Mother?"

"Helga, she will be fine. Let her keep making her clothing. Helga, there are two individuals you can trust at the registry. I do not know who they are, but they will let you know when the time is right! One last thing, your father wanted you to get admitted to the hospital where a resistance contact will provide you with information and medication. Now, you better go before you create suspicion for taking so long to get a bouquet of flowers."

I take the flowers from her and walk back to the registry. My mind is supersaturated with information and the most heartbreaking of all is Karl. I really thought he loved me. He loved me enough to use me to infiltrate the resistance. I wonder if the resistance knows that he is a snake in the long grass silently slithering to sneak up on its next victim.

I arrive back at the registry feeling that my heart has been ripped from my body. I climb the stairs trying to politely maneuver the line of people. I make it to the top of the stairs and suddenly feel lightheaded. I grab the nearest person for support and hang on to him until I feel my body go limp. My flowers drop out of my hands and tumble down the stairs. The man secures my limp body and Anna instructs him to lay me on the backroom floor.

When I awake, I am in the hospital hooked up to medical apparatuses. I look around and see a nurse hovering around me and Herr Boumer sitting on a chair with his head in his hands. I feel weak but I know that I have to telephone Olga and warn her of Karl. I try to tell her that I need to call home right now, but I have problems forming words. I am frightened and my heart is racing and I am gulping for air. The nurse quickly places an oxygen mask over my mouth and nose and gives me an injection. I must call home; I must call home; then darkness once again overtakes me.

I wake up and my room is dark. I focus my eyes, my pupils becoming as big as dinner plates. I am not alone as I see Olga slumped in the chair beside the door. She hears me stirring and comes over to my side.

"Helga, you gave us quite the scare young lady."

"Olga, I need to tell you something. I wanted to call you from the registry, but I couldn't."

"Relax Helga. I went over to Mrs. Yvo to get you more flowers and I told her that you are in the hospital. She relayed your message to me."

"How did you find out about me?"

"Herr Boumer came over and told your mother and I that you had collapsed at the registry. He offered to drive us to the hospital to see you. Your mother left a few hours ago. Don't worry she is fine! I asked one of the nurses to get one of the doctors, not Dr. Karl, to give me one of her medications. Actually, it worked out well as he asked her what she is taking and was surprised when she told him. He took her into a separate room and spoke to her and then he called me in. He did an assessment of your mother and suggested that she tries another medication, which she agreed to. When we came back into your room to check on you, Herr Boumer was here with more flowers and a huge food basket to take home. He drove your mother home with the food basket. Lukasz is keeping an eye on her and making sure that Karl does not get into the house."

"Herr Boumer is a good man, Helga".

"How can you say that as he is more Nazi than human! I can see though that he adores you, but he also adores his wife!"

"Has Karl been in?"

"Yes, he has been in, checking on you and reading your chart!"

"I never want to see that useless piece of filth again!"

Olga whispers to me, "You may have to until the resistance gets what it needs from the hospital. Be patient girl and it is important that you don't let on that you know that he is a collaborator! Helga, I am going to go inform the nurses that you are awake and then go home."

"How are you getting home?"

"Herr Boumer told me to call him, which I will after talking to the nurses."

One of my nurses comes in and turns on the light. She asks me how I am feeling and does her assessment on me. I tell her that I am hungry and thirsty and will she bring me something to drink and eat. She leaves and comes back with some water, juice, clear broth and dry bread.

"Ms. Helga, you have gone through a lot of turmoil lately. I am glad you are here where you can rest. Please eat up what I have brought you and I will be back after I check on my other patients."

As she leaves. Karl comes in to see me.

"My Helga, I am so glad you are awake. I have checked on you several times, but you were sound asleep. You didn't even respond when I gave you a kiss on your cheek. How are you feeling my love?"

"I am feeling better thank you Karl. I just want to go home!"

"I know my love. I want to take you home and cuddle with you and keep you safe. You gave me quite the scare."

"I am sorry my love, I didn't mean to."

"I know that it must be hard on you with your father's death."

"Karl, he was murdered by the Gestapo and I know they will not release his body so we can give him a proper Christian burial."

"I know darling, but not even I can't help you with that. The Gestapo will not listen to a Dutch doctor. Do you want me to try anyways?"

"No Karl, it is fine. I do not want you to be in their radar. I have lost too much already and don't want to lose you too. I can't wait until I am your wife, and we have many little Karl's and Helga's running around."

"Helga, I look forward to that also. I must go now and check on my patients. I love you and I will see you later."

"I love you also Karl."

He leaves the room and I stick my finger in my mouth, pretending to gag. My inside voice speaks to me again *Karl, I will never be your wife. I will never have your children. All I want is to shoot you between the eyes! You traitor!*

The food my nurse brings me is bland but eases my hunger pangs. My nurse comes back and asks if I enjoyed my feast. We both laugh. She sits beside me on the bed and leans toward me.

"Helga, I am your contact. I have important paperwork for you and will slip it under your bed when you go back to sleep. Also, I have medication for the resistance. I will hide the small bag under your pillow. You can give them to Olga tomorrow."

"Nurse, how long will I be in the hospital for?"

"Call me Gerta. Your doctor has recommended that you stay here for three more days. That will give us ample time to get the documents and lots of medication and medical supplies out of the hospital."

"Was my father involved in this?"

"Ms. Helga your father knew what was going on. What he did was admirable as he drew attention to himself so we could be under the Nazi's radar. He knew Karl was a collaborator so he purposely played right into Karl's hands. Helga, your father is a hero! Now take this sedative so you can have a good sleep."

The next morning when I wake up, I feel well rested. My new nurse suggests that I get up and walk around the floor with her assistance. I check underneath my pillow and I feel a bag of medication. I ask if I can delay it until Olga or my mother shows up and I will walk with them. Days really drag on in the hospital. I can't even read a good book because most have been banned!

Olga finally arrives with Lukasz. Lukasz drove Father's car. I give them what Gerta snuck into my room. I tell both of them that she works the night shift so they can arrive at around lunch time and I will have items for them. I tell Olga we need to go for a walk as I told my new nurse that I was waiting for her to arrive so we can walk together. She grabs my arm and we walk on the floor. The hospital is infested with Nazis, but we ignore them. When it is safe, she whispers in my ear that their identities have changed. We are working on changing Berta and the Katz ladies as well.

"Mother?"

"Yes, don't ask any questions here." She quietly says.

Out loud she asks me how I am feeling with my walk and several Wehrmacht soldiers look our way. I see the nurses who support the Reich giving these soldiers the salute. My new nurse is one of them. Bitch!

"I am feeling better now that I am walking. Let's turn around though before I get tired".

When we return my bland lunch is waiting for me and Lukasz signals that he has the resistance material.

"Helga, we will let you eat and rest. I will give your mother your love." Olga says.

My doctor comes in and checks on me. He says I am here for a few more days until I can show that I am healthy enough to go home. He winks at me and gives me my prescribed medication. He then digs deep into his pocket. He pulls out another two bottles and places them under my pillow.

"Ms. Helga, I will bring more medication today for you. Karl is working on another floor busy euthanizing undesirables. I will call Olga to come back to the hospital at 16:00 as I want to have a meeting with you both. This sedative will put you out, but I will get another one of resistance nurses to come in when your new nurse is gone. She is actually sexually involved with Karl."

"What?" I whisper. "For how long?"

"A long time before he met you my dear. We are planning to exterminate them when the time is right."

"Can I have the honors?"

"Yes, my dear, but act normal like you are still in love. I will be back later my dear. Enjoy your lunch and sleep well."

"I will, thank you."

I eat my lunch and lie on the bed. Karl and his love both come in to check on me. I pretend that I am asleep. They do not say a word but that suits me perfectly.

I am awakened by my doctor shaking my arm.

"Sorry, Ms. Helga, but Olga is here for our discussion."

It is decided that I will stay here until he is comfortable that I can function on my own at home. I feel like telling him, my mother and a housekeeper/cook who takes good care of me. He whispers to each of us that he and Gerta will need that amount of time to pass information and medical supplies to us.

I haven't seen Herr Boumer today and that surprises me. My irrational inner voice is saying he loves you and he will be in yet, the rational inner voice tells me that he was just being a good boss. Nothing more. He flirts with me as he is a very sexually deprived man. He is just like Karl, a wasted piece of skin!

Gerta is on duty now and digs more medication out of her pockets and slips them to Olga when she moves to the other side of my bed. My doctor instructs Gerta to watch me as I am not ready to go home yet. The doctor whispers to me to be careful and the best defense is to pretend you are sleeping. Gerta readjusts my pillow and the sheets tucked under the mattress.

"Helga, I will bring you more tonight."

Now this is my routine for the next four days. I pray and hope that the Nazis do not get suspicious. Olga has mentioned that Karl has not been around the house since Father died. Good, but I know he is up to something.

It is my last day here before I am discharged, Olga has visited me and collected the resistance stuff already. Later that morning, when I am pretending to sleep, I feel a hand under my pillow. I pretend to look startled and see that it is Karl rummaging beneath my pillow. I look at him crossly and ask him what the hell he is doing as he woke me up out of a sound sleep.

"Helga, my love, I am fluffing your pillow for you." He says with a smug look on his face. "I am making sure that my future wife is comfortable."

"Please leave now as you woke me up and I am still tired. But first, can you get me my nurse as I need a glass of water?"

"I can get that for you dear."

It takes him longer than usual to get me a glass of water. Has he gone to the nearest canal to me a glass of water? Something inside of me tells me to pretend that I am asleep. He returns and nudges me to wake up. I keep my eyes closed as if my life depends upon it. I can hear him getting frustrated with me.

"Wake up you stupid bitch. Fuck you. Drink this water and you will join you father!"

I keep my eyes closed for what seemed like hours. When I open them, I see my glass of water with a white sediment in the bottom of the glass.

"That fucker wanted to poison me!"

I can't tell my nurse as it is his lover and spy. I will play his game. I spill some water by my mouth, on my bed, and tip the glass onto the floor where it smashes. One of the nurses is walking by and hears it. She comes in and I pretend that I am convulsing!

She yells, "Get her doctor right way! This is an emergency!"

She turns me on my side and I keep trying to convulse. It takes a lot of work to act like a fish out of water. My doctor arrives and pushes the nurse out of his way. He gives her orders for medication for me. The collaborating nurse comes in all excited, trying to get involved in my treatment. He yells at her to go and get me more blankets as he doesn't want me to go into shock. When everyone who is in the room leaves, he asks me what is going on. I tell him about Karl checking underneath my pillow and how he tried to poison me. My doctor looks at a piece of the broken base of the glass and sees that white residue.

"Helga, it isn't safe for you or me and my colleague here anymore."

"How can I get out of the hospital with the hospital full of collaborators?"

"I have an idea and you will have to trust me."

My doctor asks me if I can slow down my breathing and heart rate voluntarily. I tell him not really. He gives me half of a weak sedative that will lower my heart and breathing rates and give the illusion that I am dead. He tells me that the sedative will wear off in two hours. Then we will get you, me, and the other resistance members out of the hospital. When the nurses come back, I will tell them that you stopped breathing and died.

The two nurses return and my doctor removes his stethoscope from my chest. He pulls the blankets over my head and informs them I am gone. He gives them my time of death as 16:02. He points to Karl's lover and tells her to call my house and tell Olga to come to the hospital right away.

"What about her mother?"

"Olga will have to tell her mother as she is very fragile these days with the loss of her husband and now her daughter."

He asks the nurse in charge to call Gerta into work early because we will need an extra set of hands dealing with Helga's death. He tells her that my family has recently lost Father and now with the loss of their only daughter, they will be very distraught. Plus, nurse Gerta has a good rapport with the family so that will hopefully make thing easier for them. My doctor makes sure that he follows hospital protocol. He knows that my body will be released as I am a Dutch woman. The only way it will not happen is if Karl puts his Nazi nose in it. Speak of the devil while my doctor is completing the paperwork, Karl runs into my room.

"Is it true? Is it true that my fiancé is dead?"

"Yes, it is!"

"What happened?" Karl asks sincerely.

"I think she was given the wrong medication. She was convulsing and her breathing became more and more shallow. Then she stopped breathing. I tried to revive her but, she was gone! She was such a beautiful young woman."

"Doctor, can you please check to see if her engagement ring is on her left ring finger."

My doctor retrieves the ring and gives it to Karl. He takes it and walks out without saying another word! Gerta arrives and the Doctor instructs her to stay with me until my family arrives and under no circumstances should my body be removed! He says it out loud for the benefit of the ears listening. He whispers about what happened and that they have been compromised.

When Helga and Lukasz arrive, they do not know what is going on. They believe that I am dead as that what the head nurse said. They storm into my room and are greeted by a smiling Gerta. I peek my head from under the blankets. The look on their faces is priceless as they look like they have just seen a ghost! Gerta scolds me and pulls the covers back where they belong. She whispers to them what has happened and suggests that they act like they are stricken with grief over losing me. Act 1 Scene 1- grieving relatives. They make such a commotion that the nurse in charge locates my doctor and tells him that the grieving family members could each use a sedative. They are disturbing other patients. My doctor is thankful that the nurse is loud with her request. The Nazi soldiers and other medical staff look towards the direction of the wailing. He looks at the group of gawkers and informs them that he will give them a good sedative to shut them up. He quickly goes into the medical room and grabs a bottle of sedatives for Olga and Lukasz. While there he puts a couple bottles of medicine, vials of morphine and insulin into his coat pocket. He leaves several vials behind for good measure. When he walks out of the medication room he is face to face with Karl and a Wehrmacht guard.

"What were you doing in there, Herr Doctor?"

"I was doing my job and getting medication for Ms. Helga's grieving family members. Can't you hear their wailing from here!?"

"Let me see what you have in your hands, I do not trust you!"

The doctor opens up his hand and shows him the bottle of sedatives. "You see, they are sedatives for her family members."

The soldier shrugs his shoulder and walks away. Doctor looks Karl in the eyes and whispers, "It is unfortunate that Ms. Helga trusted you to get her clean healthy water!" He pushes Karl away and continues to the wailing.

"Good job you have everyone staring at this room! I have told nosy Karl that I am giving you two sedatives. Gerta can you get a glass of water for me, quickly!"

She returns with the water and says Karl is on his way. Olga and Lukasz take just enough water to wet their lips. Karl enters the room and Olga hugs him.

"Karl, I am so sorry for your loss. We will take care of Helga and give her a proper burial."

"Actually, I am not sure that the Nazis will release her body."

Everyone is quiet until Olga questions why.

He looks at Olga and firmly states "You never question the authority of the Third Reich. Do you all understand?"

"Yes." everyone answers in harmony.

Once he was gone, my doctor states that we have to leave now. He instructs Lukasz to move his car to the far side of the building. Gerta you be the lookout for Nazi trouble. Helga get dressed and Olga take these medications I have with me. I am going to distract the Nazis at the other side of the medicine room. You all sneak out of this room and take the stairs to the outside of the building. Gerta you go with them. I know that I will not be joining you as I want to make sure that the group of you get out safely. I have a cyanide capsule in the back of my mouth. I will give you three minutes to get out of the building and then I will start aggravating the Nazis. I wish you all the best and get out of Amsterdam right away as it is going to get worse. He gives us all hugs and kisses and we see him walk toward the group of Nazis. He looks back and we are gone. All I hear is my heart racing and our feet pounding on the stairs.

Lukasz snuck out ahead of us and when we get to the far side of the hospital, we see him waiting for us at our designated spot. He somehow managed to steal a doctor's coat just in case he got stopped. Olga tries to lessen the severity of the situation, "Act 1 Scene 3 Escape from hospital Take 1."

We are able to laugh but our hearts are in our mouths as we have to get the hell away from the hospital. We don't see any check points, so all is well, so far.

"Hey everyone," I say in a cocky manner, "I raced down those stairs pretty good for a dead person!"

Gerta is sitting beside me in the back seat of the car and comments that I am an amazing woman.

"Lukasz can you please turn left on the next roadway and then right. There is an alleyway 25 meters from where I want you to drop me off. Olga, please give me all the medication and documents you have with you." She then hands each of us a cyanide pill to hide on ourselves, just in case.

"Gerta will we see you again?" I ask inquisitively.

"No dear Helga, I am going to stay in Amsterdam as long as I can. I have many disguises. I want to seductively lure German officers; use them to get information and then murder them."

"I wish I was that brave." I comment sincerely.

"Helga, you are brave. From what I understand you have been doing important work for the resistance and you sacrificed your dignity to get into the coding room. The resistance is proud of you. But always be on the guard for the snake in the grass." Gerta speaks with concern.

Gerta digs in her bag and pulls out a vial and two syringes.

"Helga, Olga, and Lukasz, I have a vial of poison for you to administer to your choice of undesirables. I am only giving you one syringe, but I am sure you will not be worried about cleanliness when you inject your enemies with them!" Gerta says with an evil look on her face. She hands me the vial and syringe and I put them deep in my purse.

Lukasz stops the car and Gerta looks at us all. "Alright my friends, we will probably never meet again. If we do, it is imperative that we do not acknowledge each other. Nazi and collaborator eyes are everywhere. Goodbye my friends."

I watch as her figure is swallowed up by the darkness of the night. I feel a lone tear trickle down my cheek. I hope and pray she seduces and kills many officers. She is a goddess in my eyes. Lukasz drives the indirect route to our house. I look forward to seeing Mother and giving her a big hug!

CHAPTER FORTY-ONE

Lukasz cautiously drives up to our house. Olga and I are scanning the dark street for any form of life or unusual vehicles. Everything looks good. Lukasz parks father's car in his usual spot. He instructs us to open and close the doors quietly. I feel like a spy sneaking up on an unsuspecting victim. In this case, I hope that we don't scare Mother too much. As we slowly walk up to our house, I cannot see any light from Mother's dressmaking room. Even with the blackout curtains I can usually see a flicker of light, like fireflies dancing in the dark. Lukasz opens the door, and we enter an eerily quiet house. Even when I come home from the registry late there is a subtle form of light in the house. The door to mother's dressmaking room is closed. After all these years, I know my way in my house, but I use the foyer wall as I walk towards the parlor, with Olga and Lukasz beside me. When we enter the parlor, we are suddenly blinded by several bright lights. I feel like a bat wanting to escape the daylight and return to the safety of the bat-house. I cannot see who is shining the lights at us but then I hear a familiar voice.

"Fraulein Helga, my love, you look amazing for a dead person!"

Fuck, its Karl.

"Darling did you miss me?" I ask him in a desperate tone.

"Yes, I missed you and your resistance friends tremendously."

My eyes adjust to the light and I see Karl sitting on father's favorite chair with a gun on his lap, he has with him two SS soldiers who are pointing their guns pointing at us.

"My, love I did not expect this type of welcoming from you."

"Fraulein, shut the fuck up. Now you, Olga, and Lukasz come over and have a seat in the parlor. First of all, I have bad news for you three. The dear doctor that assisted you at the hospital and forged your death is dead. It is unfortunate that we were unable to interrogate him as he took his own life. That is fine though as we will hunt, torture, and slaughter all of your fellow resistance members."

"But Karl, you were the one that told me you are part of the communist resistance group." I firmly state to him.

"Yes, my dear, I did. I had an idea that my father was part of the communist resistance. So, I used him to get you and I into the group. I must give my father credit as he made sure that I did not interact directly with members of the group."

"Karl, what about the names you gave Olga to give to me?"

"Oh yes, the lists. Well, those names were made up. My contact in the registry created the false census cards for me. So stupid you went ahead and did your secretive work. The individuals that were assigned those names were Nazi collaborators and they successfully infiltrated your resistance group. We have arrested several members and right now they are being interrogated by the Gestapo, one at a time in the room where your father was. By the way Helga, Lars was very smart to get you to execute him, he was a weak man and I know that he would have snapped under pressure. What we should have done is when you were in the room the Gestapo agent should have started to beat you. He would have begun singing then. Your father was a weak man!"

Those last five words stung hard. "How dare you insult my father. He is more of a man than you will ever be!"

I look at Karl with hateful eyes filled with the fires from hell. I get up from the couch and walk slowly over to him. I can feel five sets of eyes following me. I want to get close enough to take his luger. I look and he has his hand firmly on his gun, he looks at me with an evil grin on his face. I extend my arms out affectionately toward him when we are all startled by a loud sound coming from the back of the house. Karl jumps from father's chair. He looks at the two SS officers and points to where the noise came from.

"I thought you checked this house thoroughly. I know there is secret rooms and hidden panels in this house. Go see what the noise is and I will keep watch these three."

I look at Olga and Lukasz and they are as puzzled as I am.

"Karl, what have you and the Nazi pigs done with Mother? She always treated you kindly and with respect."

"Helga, I don't know where that old bitch is, but we will find her."

The SS soldiers come back and state that the back door is open.

"Fuck, who is it now?"

Karl points to one of the officers and shouts at him to radio for reinforcements. I have a bad feeling about this. The two of us will handle these three – a weak woman and an old bitch and man.

"Now you," he points to Olga, "You turn on every light in this house so we can see what the hell is going on."

He points to the other officer and instructs him to follow her and shoot her if she does not comply. "I am tired of this fucking family! Now you two don't even think of moving or I will shoot you both."

The other SS officer returns and informs Karl that reinforcements are on the way and will be here soon. I am trying to think who could have opened our back door. Mother is clearly gone. I look at Lukasz but he doesn't give me any indication with his body language.

"Karl, I have to urinate badly." He looks at me and ignores my request. "Karl, I have to urinate badly. Karl, I have to urinate badly!"

I know from the look on his face that I am irritating him.

"Shut the fuck up." he yells at me.

Again, I tell him that I have to urinate NOW.

"Herr Weinerz, take this whiney bitch up to have a piss. Do not let her out of your sight."

I rise from the couch and put my hand to my crotch indicating that I have to urinate badly. Karl sees me take my purse and tells me to drop it!

"Can I at least take my sanitary towel with me or do you prefer me to menstruate everywhere?"

"Fucking woman! Alright, watch her though."

I walk quickly up the stairs as if I don't want to urinate on myself. I get to the entrance of the lavatory and quietly ask the SS officer if he wants to watch me while I urinate and deal with menstrual blood. He shakes his head and tells me to make it quick.

I quickly remove the vial and syringe from my sanitary box. I fill the syringe full of my doctor death. The officer knocks on the door and tells me to hurry up. I have a thousand scenarios going through my mind about the current situation in my house. But I know I have to deal with the here and now, not unrealistic scenarios. I respond to Herr SS Officer in German that I will be right out. I just have severe menstrual cramps. You are lucky you're a man. I know that men view menstruation as taboo and will avoid talking about it or dealing with it. As I open the lavatory door, I act like I am keeled over in cramps. The SS officer is standing outside the door and I jab him in the leg with my syringe. He loses his balance and falls on the floor. Karl yells and asks what is going on.

I blurt out, "I fell, and the SS officer is trying to help me up."

Karl does not believe me of course and runs to the stairs. All he sees is Herr Weinerz convulsing on the floor. I run into Mother and Father's bedroom to hide.

"Fuck!" He yells for the other officer but there is no response. "I will get you, you…"

He does not finish his sentence as Lukasz has him in a chock hold and has wrestled his gun from him.

"Helga, it is safe; come out. Quickly before the other Germans arrive."

I open my parent's door and kick the lifeless SS officer and relieve him of his gun, ammunition, and grenades.

"Olga are you alright?" I yell down the stairs.

"Yes, I am thanks to this helpful man."

I wonder if it is an unknown member of the communist resistance. I walk into the parlor where Lukasz has subdued Karl and I see Doff standing beside Olga.

"Doff what are you doing here? Why?"

"Helga, darling I guess I fooled you very well, I am one of the resistance contacts at the registry. I told you that I would protect you."

He walks over and gives me a big kiss.

"Enough." Lukasz speaks sharply. "We have to decide what to do with Karl and we need to get out of here quickly."

"Lady and gentlemen, may I have the honors of terminating this piece of shit?" I ask the others.

Karl pipes up, "You do not have the guts to terminate my life. I am your fiancé!"

I look him in the eyes and shrug my shoulders. "My dear Karl, I quit being your fiancé when you removed my engagement ring from my finger while I was in the hospital."

Lukasz hands me his luger but I do not accept it. I take the vial of poison out of my purse and fill the syringe I'm holding with the fluid.

"Karl, I regret that I do not have a sterile syringe for you, but I know that all Nazis and their collaborators have the same type of blood."

As I walk over to him, he begins to squirm. "Are you afraid of dying Karl? Oh, by the way, we will find your nurse friend and her life will be terminated in the most inhumane way possible!"

I instruct Lukasz to hold him still. I actually see the terror in his eyes. I give him a smile and then jab him in the neck and we push him onto the carpet. Doff comes over and puts his arm around me and we watch as Karl convulses and takes his last breath!

Olga and Lukasz shout that we need to go now. Doff and I collect Karl's gun and we all dart out the back door. It is a bright night as it is a full moon and the stars are sparkling like diamonds on a black blanket. We hear shouting out front and we know the Nazis have showed up. I take off my light-colored jacket to reveal my dark sweater. We meander between the trees in the back of our house, the former Katz place and several neighbors I never got to know. We know that the area will be crawling with Nazis, but we keep moving until we reach a roadway. Doff's black sedan is sitting there and his driver is waiting for us. Lukasz hides in the trunk and Olga and I lie on the floor in the back seat. Doff covers us with a blanket and we speed off. Goodbye my house. Goodbye Mother, wherever she is!

CHAPTER FORTY-TWO

W e make it safely to wherever we are going. I know that Doff is stopped by a checkpoint, but he is not interrogated once the Wehrmacht soldiers see his credentials. We arrive at our destination and are shuffled into a house.

"Welcome to my home. Please come in and relax!" He says.

I look around his house and see it is modest, not luxurious by any means.

"Helga, could you please help me with making some tea and food?"

"Sure."

"Olga and Lukasz, you do your thing, and we will come get you when the food is ready, and we will bring you a warm cup of tea."

Do their thing? What the hell is he talking about.

"Wait Olga, I want to know about Mother, the Katz women and the photographer."

Doff looks at me sincerely and tells me not to worry as everyone is fine. Great, I have more questions for him. I go into the kitchen to heat water for the tea. Doff joins me and begins to grab food for us to cook. I am feeling a little cheeky.

"Herr Boumer, where is your wife? Should she not be preparing the tea and food for your guests?"

He walks up to me and puts his arms around me and confesses that he does not have a wife or a girlfriend.

"Herr Boumer, is there any truth to you at all? Is your whole life a façade?"

"Fraulein Helga, the truth is I am in love with you. I fell in love with you when I first set eyes on you. Your feisty spirit and beauty enticed me."

"When did you become part of the resistance?"

"I have always had a hatred for the Nazis, but I had to play the pro-Nazi game to stay alive. I had several meetings with Ared and Himmler and they outlined the plans for the Germanization of this country. I listened to them callously and sarcastically laughed at the demise of the undesirables they would exterminate like filthy rats. My secretary, the kind older lady, took me under her resistance wing."

"Your secretary?" I say in disbelief.

"Yes, and don't underestimate her. She is very efficient in slicing one's throat with the knife she carries in her handbag!"

"Who reported Leos?"

Leos and Leike were part of another resistance group. Through my connections I met Mrs. V. and she expressed her concern about their sloppiness, they were toxic for any other resistance group. I had to agree with her as Leos did not hide the fact that she was stealing cards from the registry. Mrs. V. and I decided that these two women were a liability and need to be exterminated."

"Wow! Karl wanted me to avoid those two women!"

"It doesn't surprise me as they were already caught in the Gestapo trap and I know that he wanted you to lead him to other members of the communist resistance. I know that he stated that he was part of the resistance, but it was all an act, he was using you to lead him to the resistance group leaders. I know for a fact that the communist resistance group were already suspicious of him. Helga, if you had not killed him, they would have sent someone else!"

"Well, it gives me great satisfaction that I had the privilege of terminating his life!"

"Helga, I never want to get on your bad side." Doff comments with a smile.

"Doff, Karl also leaked to me that there was a collaborator in the registry. Do you have any idea who it is?"

"I have a suspicion it could be Anna or Marie. The best way I can test them is to divide my workers into small groups and bring them into my office. I will announce that you are dead. I will watch their reactions to my responses. A good collaborator can very easily mimic her reactions. So, I will add fuel to the fire. I will have all the workers in the back office and have you come into the office. My secretary has eyes like a hawk, and she can watch the reactions for me also. Then we will have to get you the hell out of the registry before you are arrested. You do realize that you are a wanted woman. And as a side note, I want you also!"

"Doff, I have so many questions as my world has been turned upside down and inside out!"

"I know Helga, but all of our emotions are raw. We will answer all of your questions and fill in the blanks for you soon. Trust me when I say that Berta and the Katz women are safe."

I walk over and give me a hug and a big deep kiss. I put my right hand at the front of his pants and stroke his pants as his penis bulges to be free.

"Mmmm I still have it. Doff."

He looks at me in surprise and disbelief. "Helga, you drive me crazy my beautiful woman!"

"Am I your woman Herr Boumer?"

"Yes, my Helga! Now we need to make tea for five people."

"Five people?"

"Yes, my dear, the photography man has joined us!"

"The last time I heard about photography man he was hiding in Lukasz's cabin probably under the floorboard with the Katz women. I.." Then I stop my sentence. Remember they will talk later, do not push the issue!

I rummage through Doff's kitchen area and find the pot to heat the water for tea and ample food to make a great feast for dinner. I make a strong pot of tea which Doff takes to the others. I inform him that we, he and I, will be making a one pot meal with meat and vegetables. This delicious concoction will be served with fresh bread. I added that the two cooks should also enjoy a glass of bubbly while we are working. Doff looks at me with a twinkle in his eye and seductive grin on his face.

Ms. Helga, I have several bottles of Clio that we grabbed from your father's collection. I have to inform you that I do not own the proper Clio glasses, all I can offer you is a larger wine glass best suited for red wine. Is that satisfactory?"

"Yes, it is Doff, but be sure to fill the glasses full of Clio as I enjoy a great glass of bubbly with a great man!"

I watch as he pops the Clio's cork and it hits the ceiling with a thud. I comment "Music to my ears baby." as I put my arms around him.

"Helga, you are such a tease."

"Doff, are we safe here?" I ask in a concerned voice.

"Helga, this will be the last meal that we all have together. It is too dangerous and I am sure that Karl's death will lead the Gestapo to you and then to me."

"Doff, do you have any spices I can add to dinner?"

"Spices?" he laughs.

"Guess not, I will add extra onion then."

"Oh, I think I have some on the lower shelf."

"I will check." As I bend down looking for the onion I see him looking at my bottom out of the corner of my eye.

"Herr Boumer, you tricked me. You just wanted to stare at my bottom!"

"You caught me Fraulein, I enjoy watching your bottom."

"Are you flirting with me?"

"Of course!"

Olga comes out of the room where she is working with Lukasz and photography man and joins us. "We have completed our work and now we can relax. Do you two want to see what we have accomplished?"

"That would be great," I answer.

"The deal is we will bring out our work if you share the bubby with the three of us."

I grab another three of the red wine glasses and Doff pours the left-over wine in our bottle into one of the glasses. We laugh as it only fills one third of the wine glass. Pop! There goes another cork, and we fill the glasses with ample bubbly. The savory smells of the meat and vegetables cooking permeates the house. Olga comments that I am taking over her job! Doff grabs a couple kitchen chairs as we converge in the parlor. Olga hands each of us our new birth certificates, census and identification cards. She points out that I am now Professor Arabella Venderpaz and Doff is Aart Venderpaz. We are a married couple. I am a professor of Romance Languages and Doff is a plant manager. She instructs us to memorize our new identities as our lives will depend on it.

Olga speaks first with a serious look on her face. "Helga, your mother and the Katz women are on their way to Switzerland. I shouldn't be telling you this just in case you get captured but they are travelling to Brussels and then into France. Berta and I exchanged most of her dresses on the black market for supplies. She did save a couple dresses for you. She took some of her heirloom jewelry and family pictures with her. The Katz women took family heirlooms, pictures, and a few mementoes. They have a long journey ahead of them and I made sure that they packed practical clothing and shoes. Berta was disappointed that she could not bring her fancy high heels. I told her that that are not very practical when you have to climb up a mountain. The rest of the valuables, including the Katz's beautiful paintings are hidden with a trustworthy Dutch friend. I have given Berta, and I will give you and Doff, the names and addresses of these people. Helga, the last words that Berta spoke to us was that she was sorry and that she will wait for you in Switzerland."

I have tears in my eyes as I think of Mother travelling in uncertainty. I remember her as an irrational woman. I ask Olga about her state of mind and she reminds me that when I was in the hospital she met with my doctor and he changed her medication. She was previously misdiagnosed which caused her to act crazy!

"Now we need to focus." Doff pipes up. "Tomorrow, my driver will drop Olga and Lukasz off at their assigned safehouses. You both know that you two will be together once it is deemed safe to move you. Mr. Photography Man, you and your equipment and supplies will enjoy a comfortable ride in the trunk of my sedan. You will be going to another safe house where you will work on forging documents. Helga, you will stay hidden here with me and my driver until I figure out who the Nazi collaborators are at the registry. This is all up in the air. If I find that it is unsafe, I will give you a code word and you will go to a safehouse. Right now, I think it is important that we relax and enjoy our bubbly and the amazing meal that Helga is preparing for us." Doff pops another cork and we sit around enjoying each other's company and light talk.

"Do you know what I am not going to miss?" I ask. "I will not miss a Nazi Christmas where Christmas hymns are forbidden and the swastika is at the top of the tree."

"I won't miss making Christmas cookies in the shape of birds, wheels, and swastikas." Laughs Olga.

Lukasz, who is a man of few words, comments, "What annoyed me the most was the fact that the Nazis wanted to make Christmas a National Socialist Celebration. The ones close to the Hitler advertised that Christmas eve has nothing to do with the birth of Christ but the rebirth of the sun as it sets solstice. We are expected to replace Jesus as our savior with Adolf Hitler as our savior!"

We all nod in agreement and I comment that the first thing I want to do when I reach freedom is sing a Christmas hymn! I excuse myself as I have to check on dinner and set the table. I look at my friends sitting in the parlor and hope to see them again soon, alive. Doff decides to join me in the kitchen. We laugh and flirt with each other as we get dinner ready. Doff suddenly changes his demeanor like the weather in the Atlantic Ocean.

"Mrs. Arabella Venderpaz I love you so much!"

"Mr. Venderpaz, I love you also."

The sparks are flying between us and I know that after tonight I will no longer be a virgin!

The table is set for six, including Doff's driver, and more corks are popped! The meal is delicious.

"My friends this is our last dinner together. We will be dispersed like snowflakes in the wind. Hopefully, we can all meet after the war. I know that Berta will meet Helga in Switzerland. I imagine that the Katz women will find their own unique destinations once they reach freedom. Olga and Lukasz where do you want your final destination to be?" Doff asks.

"I would like to look for my mother in Russia."

Lukasz comments, "I will join you Olga if you will allow me. I am very fond of you." Lukasz pushes his chair back and walks and gives Olga a big kiss.

"Hey, none of that at the table now!" I exclaim.

Doff flirtatious says, "Really?" and walks over and begins to explore my mouth with his tongue before turning to the photographer.

"What about you Mr. Photography man?"

"I will stay in Amsterdam as long as I can, then I will visit my sister in Rotterdam. I will get to see my nieces and nephews. My sister has five children so far, I think she wants to repopulate Rotterdam!"

Doff pours us another glass of wine and I see that everyone's eyes, including mine are getting sleepy. I ask Doff's driver what he will be doing? He surprises me when he states that he will continue working with the underground but now as a full-time radio operator. The table is cleared, and the last glass of wine is gulped down. It is earlier in the night but we all have an early morning and everyone needs to be well rested. Doff suggests that the men take turns staying awake and watching for unexpected visitors. The ladies get to sleep. Lukasz volunteers for first shift. The group scatters and it is only Doff and I.

"Ms. Helga you can either sleep with me or I can have an uncomfortable sleep on the couch."

I grab his hand and say the bed. We venture up the stairs to his bedroom. I wash up and apologize for not having a night gown. I join him in bed with my cold skin touching his warm body. He lies on his back and I lie on his arm. He gently touches my arm and it feels like a gentle wave soothing my body. He looks at me and I am sound asleep. He kisses my forehead and then he nestles in for a special sleep until it is his turn to guard his, hopefully, future wife!

CHAPTER FORTY-THREE

I awaken well rested and yes, I am still a virgin, except for his finger penetration in his office. There is a fury of activity in the house below. I quickly get dressed and am greeted by the aroma of fresh real coffee and eggs cooking. Olga and Lukasz have their packed bags by the front of the door. Mr. Photography has his bags further back in the line. The meal is consumed at the table, on the couch, or wherever someone plopped their butt. I look around and I don't see Doff.

"Where is Doff and his driver?" I ask with a concerned voice.

Olga explains that Doff went into work early before the workers arrived. He and his driver are on a mission to steal as many blank census and identification cards as he can. He will bribe the Wehrmacht guards at the entrance of the registry. He plans for him and his driver to make several trips in and out of the registry. His driver will come back here and pick up Lukasz and I and we will go to our designated safe houses with the stolen cards.

Twenty minutes later Doff's driver arrives and instructs Olga and Lukasz to exit the back door as there are too many eyes out front. He agrees to meet them both at a side street two blocks over. I look at my family members with tears in my eyes. We hug and Olga whispers in my ear to join her and Lukasz in Russia. A communist belongs in Russia not Switzerland. I agree and she tells me the name of the little village she will meet me at when the war is over. After many hugs, kisses, and well wishes Doff's driver tells them to move their asses! As the door closes behind Lukasz, I pray that my family will survive the war.

I walk out to the kitchen with my tears flowing from my eyes and blurring my vision. I look at Mr. Photography man and he is pacing back and forth. He has a distant look in his eyes as he looks like he is in a trance. I clear the tears from my eyes and I study him curiously.

"Why is he so nervous?" I ask myself and wonder if I should ask him if he is alright. My concentration is broken by the telephone ringing. I walk over to answer it and notice Photography man is following me. I answer the telephone and it is Doff.

"Run, Photography is a collaborator!"

I hang up, turn around, and he is standing in front of me. "Where do you think you are going Fraulein? My Gestapo friends want to talk to you."

He reaches out to grab my shoulders and I kick him in the groin. He drops to the ground but quickly regains his composure. I grab my purse from the hallway chair and see that he is coming at me again. I throw the chair at him and run out the back door. It is daylight and I don't know where to go. I don't know the neighborhood. I am lost. I hear him yell in German that I have escaped through the back.

"Quick get her as she can't run that fast." I hear him scream.

I am only about one hundred meters from the sound of boots hitting the ground. I have to find a place to hide. I run towards a canal and can see the soldiers behind me. I know that the Nazis will check the boats for me. I run past the boats into a thick stand of pine trees. I crouch down and watch the Nazis search the boats for me. I wander through the trees and try to get as much distance as possible between me and the Nazis. I know that I cannot go to Yvo or any other resistance members as they may be under surveillance or in custody. I finally find a little cabin off the beaten track. I see smoke coming out of the chimney, so I assume someone is home. But is this person pro-Nazi? I am hungry, exhausted, and know the sun will soon be setting as the air has a bite to it. They have a wood pile, so I decide to make myself a little wooden fortress to protect me from the cold night breeze and the Nazis. As I attempt to build my little fortress, the owner comes out and yells "Who is there?". The last thing I need is for them to call the police as I am a wanted fugitive. I walk away from the wood pile towards the owner. I explain that I was trying to build a place to sleep tonight. He asks me if I am running from the Nazis. I tell him I am. He puts his arm around me and tells me that I can stay the night with him and his wife. I walk into the little cabin and I see a star of David on the wall.

"Yes, young lady we are Jewish."

I speak to them in Yiddish and explain my situation to them. His wife tells me to sit and that she has soup for me. I ask them if they have a telephone. They don't but a neighbor two hundred meters down the road does. I inform them that I need to call the registry and see if Doff has been arrested. The couple suggests that I talk to the neighbors in the morning to see if they want to put themselves at risk. Noa, Jacob's wife, heats water for me to clean up in. She offers me one of her night gowns and their bed to sleep in. I object, but they insist that I need a good night's sleep. I thank them and go to bed feeling free for another night.

In the morning, they prepare eggs and tea for me. I know that they are very poor. I reach in my purse and give them my ration cards. They object, but I tell them that I am leaving Amsterdam and I won't need them. After breakfast I walk over to the neighbors' house to see if I can use the telephone. A young child answers and I ask to speak to her mother and father. She informs me that her daddy was taken by the Germans. My heart sinks as I look at her little innocent blue eyes and think how the Nazis have destroyed her innocence. Her mother comes to the door and I whisper my situation, so the little girl won't hear me. She welcomes me to use her telephone, but I warn her about the dangers.

"It is fine young lady as Betje and I are going to Mook where my sister lives."

"Here," I hand her one hundred guiders. "For you and Betje."

She thanks me and leaves me alone to make my telephone call.

A quiet voice answers "Hello" and I tell her who it is. She whispers that Doff was captured by the Nazis and told her that if she got in contact with me, she was to tell me to go to safehouse and he will meet me in the Russian village with the others. I question what she is going to do, and she states that she is an old woman and knows that she could not withstand any form of torture. She will take her tablet once we are done talking.

Her final words to me are, "Doff loves you. The resistance is working on helping him escape. Love him as he loves you. You are very special Helga."

She hangs up and I know that she will be gone in a few minutes. I fight back my tears as I thank the Dutch lady and Betje. I walk back to the kind Jewish family and tell them I will be going. Before I leave, I ask them if they would like a cyanide capsule each, just in case. They look at each other and smile.

"Thank you, Ms. Helga. We want to die by our own hands not by the German hands."

We hug and cry and I head out in the warm Amsterdam sun, travelling the most indirect route to my safehouse. As I am walking, I think of how effective the Germans have been in distorting my love of nature. I used to love listening to the patter of rain hitting my window, I used to look forward to the light shows and claps of thunder. As a child, mother and father told me that when you heard the bang of the thunder clouds you can time the strike of the lightening. I used to be fascinated and loved to guess how far the lightning strike was from our home. The dangers and beauty of nature.

Now, the beauty of nature has been modified by the ugliness of the Nazis. The pat pats of rain have been replaced by the shots fired by German Karabinder 98K (K98K) rifles; the former lightening show is now bombs exploding and lights emitted when the K98Ks are fired at night. These shots are immediately, in most cases, followed by a high-pitched scream. The lightning strikes are gone until I reach freedom, until I am with my Doff!